I0626854

GOD SENT AN ANGEL

J.D. WALTON

GOD SENT AN ANGEL

DEDICATION

For our parents. A book we hope they read, enjoy, and most of all, are proud we wrote. Our undying love.

Throughout adversity God's glory is manifested.

CHAPTER ONE

1990

SCREAMS BOUNCED OFF the walls of the eight-bedroom colonial mansion as everyone gathered anxiously around Anna during the delivery of her first child.

The advanced labor caused her excruciating pain and the midwife's insistence for her to push harder only added to the discomfort. Yet, she felt subdued as her twenty-nine-year-old husband, John, gripped her hand.

She knew she could endure anything for him. Even if she tried, she could not contain her affection. His love was so infectious that she was incapable of not touching him anytime they were in close proximity. Today, his touch gave her strength, but the very first day they met, her touch saved his life.

At twenty-two, John was like any other wild frat boy who roamed around the Ole Miss campus. That year, the now-classic comedy film,

Animal House, debuted and fueled him and his Greek brothers to be even more rambunctious.

Anna's father worked hard, but his blue-collar wages were not enough for him to set up a college fund. Without the option of higher education, at nineteen, Anna opted to be a first responder.

The job came naturally because she had a giving heart and knew how to react in moments of crisis. At any minute, a fresh challenge arose and kept her adrenaline rushing. Happy endings motivated her to give a hundred percent every day. She felt God used her as a vessel to save lives and prevent tragedies.

One night an emergency call was dispatched to her crew. A snake had bitten a frat boy when a magic trick went wrong at an Ole Miss party.

"In there!" College kids pointed as the crew arrived at the scene of the accident.

The first responders maneuvered through the crowd of students who partied on the front lawn wearing togas and flower crowns.

Once inside the frat house, she and her team found a guy laid out on a sofa covered in beer cans, who screamed at the top of his lungs, "I'm gonna die!"

Anna rushed to his side and pushed the mop of blonde strands that framed his blue eyes back. She could not help noticing that they were the same striking glacier color as the water bottle caps that sat on the table behind him.

When his gaze met hers, he was drawn to her green eyes. They were breathtaking and captured her vibrant soul. The iris was lush hues of the forest, while the flecks encompassed dark moss.

"You're gonna be just fine," she assured him. "The snake isn't venomous even though this is one ugly bite."

The more he looked into her earthy olive eyes, he felt as though he were grass that had been replenished after a brutal, unforgiving winter and she was the sun giving him all the nutrients he needed.

"Promise me you won't swear when I pour this alcohol over the laceration because this will burn like H-E double hockey sticks," she sweetly said while cleaning the wound.

When she smiled, the young man could not ignore the strong resemblance she bore to his latest celebrity crush, Olivia Newton-John. The star's posters covered the frat house along with Farrah Fawcett, Lynda Carter, and Suzanne Somers.

"Are you okay?" Anna asked, mistaking his goofy stare for discomfort.

"Yeah, I'm fine," he slowly answered as she finished wrapping the bandage.

"Okay, we will take you in for further examination just to be on the safe side," she informed him.

"You are the most beautiful woman I have ever seen," he mumbled as two other first responders came over to lift him onto the stretcher.

"What did you say?" She innocently asked.

"Um…" he hesitated and became self-conscious as he realized everyone stared at him. "Um..I have...um...two tickets for the Bee Gees concert this weekend and...I...um...wanted to know if you'd like to go with me."

"Only if John Travolta will be there wearing a white suit and you promise to go to church with me the next day," she laughed.

Her response and his beer guzzling frat brothers teasing him only made his pursuit more relentless.

"C'mon, I'm only trying to pay you back for saving my life," he pleaded as he laid on the stretcher.

"I don't even know your name," she blushed.

"John."

"Let me guess, your last name is Travolta," she sarcastically said.

"I would say yes, if that would make you go out with me," he laughed. "No, really, my name is John Monroe and my brothers can all vouch that I am a nice guy," he smiled expecting his charm to win her over.

As she amusingly looked at him, one of his frat brothers handed her a fat magic marker and a notebook. She smiled as she wrote her name, number, and the address of her church. She also included a smiley face with the message "don't be late."

His frat brothers who had been spectators rejoiced as though they were commentators at a football game when she handed the notebook back.

They went to that concert and John did attend church service the next day with Anna. That first date turned into many and soon after they vowed they'd spend the rest of their lives with each other.

Now, beads of sweat covered Anna's pale face as she squeezed John's hand harder each time the contractions intensified.

"Here the baby comes!" The midwife joyously said before her tone changed to one of dread. "This is a breech baby!"

"What does that mean?!?" John demanded as his parents rushed by his side.

"Anna has placenta previa. She needs emergency help or she won't make it!" The midwife panicked.

As Anna's father dialed 9-1-1, her mother swore up and down how much of a terrible idea it was to have a natural birth at home.

"Honey, are you okay?" John tried to sound normal as her screams reached new decibels.

"I have to have this baby!" She said as she breathed with closed eyes.

For fifteen minutes straight, Anna's guttural grunts filled the mansion as the midwife demanded she push.

In seconds, a tiny life landed in the midwife's hands. The great moment everyone waited for had arrived. She looked over the baby and announced it was a healthy girl. A teeny cry escaped the baby's mouth as the midwife informed the family it was a girl.

Everything felt surreal to John as she walked the baby over to him. When he looked into the baby's shiny budding eyes, he cried. All at once he became aware of so many beautiful emotions about the new consciousness he held in his arms.

Both their parents grabbed instant cameras to take pictures of their first grandchild. Anna laid back in the bed, exhausted from the labor, but mustered up a faint smile as she watched her husband hold the child she so desperately wanted to give him.

"Thank you, Anna," his voice cracked as he walked towards her with the baby, so they could bond. "I love you so much."

"Name her, Sarah," she drowsily said as he gazed into her eyes.

Before he could place the baby in her arms, she mouthed the words; 'I love you.' A lone tear traced down her cheek as she grabbed his arm and trembled, "I don't have that much time, John."

"Anna!" He yelled out in a panic state. "Help! Where's the ambulance?! Why isn't anyone doing anything?!"

"It's okay, John," she murmured. "Our precious Sarah has you and I have no doubt you'll be a great father."

"Babe, I'm getting you help now," he cried.

The paramedics rushed the bedroom, but she had already fallen unconscious. Her mother grabbed the newborn from John's arms as the medical team moved him out of the way in efforts to save Anna.

"She is going into cardiac arrest!" One of the paramedics shouted.

"Do something!!!" John demanded.

"They're trying, son," his father said to calm him down.

"We have to transport this patient to an emergency medical facility for advanced life support," one of them instructed the family.

"That's my wife! You gotta save her!" He screamed helplessly as tears poured from his eyes.

CHAPTER TWO

JOHN DID NOT realize that his father had driven him home from Northside hospital. The world turned into a blur, and so did all the sounds. The taste. The smell. Everything was dismal.

Tears burst forth like water from a dam, and spilled down his face. "I can't believe Anna is gone," he said as his chin trembled uncontrollably as though he were a small child.

"You're gonna be okay, son," his father, Bill, said as he patted him on the back and guided him to the living room.

Bill's words made no difference at all as they entered the nicely decorated room that smelled like the fresh flowers Anna carried in her wedding bouquet.

On the walls, framed photographs captured her smile. She was so beautiful. The woman of his dreams. The threads of every happy memory with his wife he could recall unraveled in his mind.

"By the grace of God, my first grandchild survived the tragedy of today. It's gonna be tough son, but you'll get through this," his father asserted as he fixed himself a drink at the bar.

"By the grace of God?" John repeated in disgust

as he grabbed a bottle of Jack Daniels. "Where was His grace today when He allowed Anna to die?! Where was her luck?!"

"Son, that's no way to talk," his father firmly responded.

"I can't believe she's gone, dad," he sobbed as he guzzled whiskey straight out of the bottle. "I told her having a home birth was too experimental and risky, but when Anna wants something she has a good way of convincing me it best. I can't believe it. I wanna be with her. I vowed I'd never leave her. Never!"

"Son, you're talking crazy and you ain't even drunk yet," Bill said alarmed. "Maybe it's best if you come home with me tonight. You know your mama wants you there."

"I'm not a child!" John snapped.

"I don't care how old you are, boy. Don't you ever take that tone with me," his father minced words. "Now, I realize it's been an awful day. Anna was a worthwhile girl, and I'm sure she wouldn't want you behaving this way."

"It hasn't even been twenty four hours and you're already referring to her in the past tense!" John shouted. "Don't you dare speak Anna's name! You barely even knew her! If I knew this was the price of having a child, I would have -"

"That's enough, son!" Bill interrupted as he picked up a visible firearm out of fear John would inflict harm on himself. "Monroe men aren't weak and I don't want you to do nothing stupid. Be rational. We've got a company to run, and you're now responsible for a tiny creature who shares our blood. Life ain't fair. It's all about the luck of the draw. I've always taught you that. I'm gonna see to it, that this house is filled with everything my granddaughter needs."

John stared blankly which frustrated Bill. "Do you hear me talkin' to you?!" He yelled.

"With all due respect, dad, I think it's best you leave," John stated before pouring more Jack Daniels down his throat.

His father shook his head out of disappointment, uncertainty, and disgust. "Just remember you have a daughter. Me and your mama will look after her until you get yourself together."

John groaned with an attitude of irreverence towards his father as Bill left the house.

With two bottles of Jack Daniels in hand, he stomped up the stairs like a madman. Once inside his bedroom he let out raw cries of hysteria. "Anna!!! I can't do this alone! You can't do this to me!"

Any unmounted object was fair game as he destroyed the place. He tripped and crashed on top of their bed where his nose smelled a scent that was all too familiar. He laid down in a fetal position and grabbed a handful of sheets and wept. His soul was tortured. He wanted nothing more than to have his wife alive.

The next ten days were obscure for John Monroe. He wrapped himself in the covers and only got out of bed to relieve himself. He did not know if he lost his mind or dreamed of the cruelest nightmares. Life as he knew it had vanished before his eyes. Pain was all that was left. Enough pain to break him. Enough pain to change him beyond recognition.

*Grief is invisible, subjective, and open to dis-
pute unless it is one's own suffering. It
is cruelty of life that a heart can keep on
beating even after it has been broken in two.*

CHAPTER THREE

1999

OVER THE YEARS, John found substantial success in the family's annuity business, Better-Life Insurance. He earned more money than the average person's lifetime net worth, but it did not make him happy. Year after year he was featured on the Richest Eligible Bachelors of Georgia list. Women made romantic advances towards him, but he was never interested. In fact, nothing excited him. As far as he was concerned, no woman could ever take Anna's place.

The mansion had an open invitation to family and friends when Anna was alive. Now in her absence, it was uninviting. Her memory loomed over the house and created a coldness instead of emitting the warmth she always radiated.

One by one, every servant quit after Anna's death because he completely shut down. The household staff could no longer tolerate his constant rudeness and micromanaging. Even when Sarah took her first steps with the nanny, he went unphased. It seemed he did not care about anyone or anything, including his daughter.

Yet, he needed help raising her, so he had to hire a nanny, which is the reason he sat in his study reviewing resumes. The cold room was washed-out in creams and pale blues. Books filled the shelves to give the appearance he was an avid reader, but really they collected dust.

Ten women had shown up to his house for an interview. He was confident one of these applicants could care for a nine-year-old.

As he stood to call the first candidate into the room, his phone rang and he answered, "Hello, Monroe residence."

"Hey, this is Rachel, from Nanny Rescue Agency, and I was calling to notify you that I am stuck in bumper to bumper traffic on I-285."

"And you're telling me this because?" He quipped.

"This is John Monroe, right?"

"It's the name I've answered to all my life and if you've done your homework, you'd know I'm a very busy man and I don't have time to waste," he replied.

"Yes, indeed. I know punctuality is one of your core principles, so that's why I wanted to inform you I'm on my way to the interview, but being that I am in a sea of cars I can't give you an approximation of my arrival. I just know I'm gonna be a tad bit late," the woman stated undefeated by John's nasty tone.

"Late?" He sarcastically repeated.

"No use in crying over spilled milk or in this case Atlanta traffic," she joked, trying to lighten the mood. "I try to be on time for –"

"Ma'am I hate to break it to you," he interjected. "But, time kills deals."

"But, sir, I really need this job," she desperately replied.

"And my daughter really needs a nanny and I have ten women who were prompt and are waiting in the next room, so you won't be needed," he said as he was about to press the red button on the cordless phone.

"Wait!!!" Rachel screeched. "I'll work the first month free, to show you my worth."

"The first month free?" John repeated after a brief hesitation.

"Yes," Rachel eagerly agreed.

"You have the job. I'll see you shortly."

CHAPTER FOUR

"MOVE IT!" RACHEL screamed in excitement as she honked the horn of her Honda Accord.

She jammed out to her favorite song, "I Want It That Way" by the Backstreet Boys as she reached for her Nokia cell phone to share the delightful news with her father.

At great expense, her father had always provided all that she needed. He was a loving parent and had a huge desire to have a vital relationship with all of his children. No matter the circumstance, she always knew she could depend on him.

"Daddy, I got my first client!" She screamed.

"I knew you would, but the hard part hasn't even come yet," he said.

"What do you mean, daddy?" She asked.

"Are you ready to be actively involved with this child's life?" He questioned.

"C'mon daddy. You know I love kids," she said with a warm joy.

"Sweetheart, you told me the father was a widower, so you have to prepare for if the child rejects your affection," he explained.

"It will be a task for sure. Not to mention I have to deal with her father being obnoxious, arrogant, bitter... Shall I continue?" She vented.

"Well, I guess he made a strong first impression on you," her father chuckled. "He may seem tough, but grief has a way of changing people. You are one of my children with a firm sense of direction and I know you will make me proud."

Her father was a wise man and was typically always right with his assessment of any situation. She noted his advice because she knew he would never lead her astray.

"I love you," her dad said as he had an incoming call.

"I love you, too."

CHAPTER FIVE

"WHO'S THAT?" SARAH asked aloud, not expecting an answer.

"She's our new substitute," her classmate, Slade, replied.

Their teacher, Mrs. Rose, had arranged the desk of twenty energetic fourth graders into groups of five that comprised two girls and two boys.

"How do you know?" Sarah questioned in a smarty-pants tone.

"Mrs. Rose called everyone's parents' last night and let them know she would be out for two weeks," Bella replied.

"Didn't your mom tell you?" Tommy, another classmate asked.

"She doesn't have a mom stupid!" Slade blurted.

"What about your dad?" Bella asked. "Didn't he tell you?"

Too embarrassed to answer Sarah shook her head no.

"Look at this," Bella said, absentmindedly changing the topic as children often did.

"Yay, you got one!" Sarah said excitedly as she looked at her friend's egg-shaped Tamagotchi.

The virtual pet with lo-fi graphics had swept

the nation. Like most elementary-aged kids, Sarah and Bella were obsessed with the toy. Sarah named all six of her Tamagotchis and carried them with her everywhere. She needed to lavish them with the constant love and attention she never received.

Out of her right corduroy pants pocket, she pulled out her pink and blue virtual pet, which she had named Ariel after her favorite Disney character.

"Let's feed them breakfast!" Bella suggested.

"Good idea!" Sarah agreed.

As Sarah fiddled with the toy buttons, she ran her fingers across the hard shell back that Ariel existed within. She did not realize that taking care of her digital pet was making an enemy out of the substitute teacher.

Chapter Six

FINALLY, WHAT SEEMED to be the longest trek known to mankind ended as Rachel's Goodyear tires drove on top of a cobblestone road surrounded by rhododendron bushes.

It took her two miles to reach a wrought-iron gate. She could not believe the view as she buzzed the intercom to be let into the estate. The grounds were meticulous and the home looked like something out of a storybook.

After she parked in the driveway, she rang the doorbell which proved to be yet another waiting process as John took his sweet time to open the door.

"Hello, Mr. Monroe," she warmly greeted him.

He blankly stared at her without returning the nicety. After a few seconds of awkward silence, she asked, "Um, is there a problem?"

"Well, I expected to see the nanny I hired for my daughter," he replied as he looked over her head and out the door wondering where the woman could be.

"She is her and I am she," she said with a smile that showcased her perfectly aligned teeth. "I am Rachel."

John's eyebrows slightly raised as she saw herself inside.

"Hmmm… I think there must be a mixup," he said on edge. "In the ad, I specifically stated that the nanny must have a degree in child psychology, the culinary skills of a Michelin-starred chef, the talent to horse ride, fluency in at least three languages, and excel in playing two instruments. I don't recall your resume detailing all those things."

""The resume that you're referencing does an excellent job of capturing how I am not Mary Poppins," she sarcastically commented. With a grin, she added, "But, I can see that you are pleasantly surprised by my arrival. If I was unqualified, we both know you wouldn't have called me for an interview."

"I'm not trying to seem rude or anything, but there are certain job requirements that I strongly don't believe you are qualified for," he countered.

His remark took her by surprise and she tried her best not to frown. "My CV boasts an impressive range of skills, so if I may dare ask, exactly what type of specifications do you consider me unqualified for?"

"You clearly haven't noticed that I'm white, and you are black," he sarcastically answered.

"Why, yes," she responded as irony lurked from her lips and eyes. "The planet is full of people who are various shades with unique backgrounds. So what is the problem?"

He let out a hearty, condescending laugh. "The problem is that I don't know jack squat about how to do a black girl's hair and I'm quite sure you could say the same about a white girl's hair. I'm not paying you $100K a year if you can't do the bare essentials."

She was ready to walk away, but she practiced patience and forgiveness as her father had taught her.

"Mr. Monroe" she sighed. "Money is not the motive for why I do my job. Not to mention, I've been working with children of all races and doing their hair for a long time. It's just hair, not rocket science" With a frosty smile she added, "If it would ease your preconceived opinion, I can schedule her weekly hair appointments."

"Now, why would I do that if that task is built into your salary?"

"Well, I guess you'll have to trust me then," Rachel said in the most optimistic tone.

"Lady, I don't put trust in no person or thing," he slyly responded.

CHAPTER SEVEN

AS JOHN GAVE Rachel a tour of his extravagant mansion, she observed that although the house was nice, it needed an interior makeover because much of the furniture looked dated. She remembered that her father once told her that the upkeep of a home speaks volumes about the owner. If it was a mess, more than likely, the person's life was not together.

"So, where are you from? I don't detect a southern accent," John dubiously asked as they walked from room to room.

"My family is from all over," Rachel casually responded.

His skeptical gaze did not go unnoticed. It was an aloof stare filled with judgment.

"The build of your walls and the install of the floors is beautiful," she commented as she examined the home.

"Thanks," he replied. "You say that as though you're an expert."

"By no means am I an expert," she humbly stated. "But some relatives taught me a thing or two about how to use a toolbox."

"You just don't strike me as the type," he said

to justify his comment. "I would have never guessed."

"Do not judge, and you will not be judged," she cleverly replied.

He changed the subject as he escorted her to her bedroom. He informed her that she would be required to pick Sarah up from school in one of the family's vehicles, and clean the house.

"Wait a minute," Rachel cut him off. "I'm not a maid, so I suggest you hire one."

"Excuse me, but that is exactly what I stated in the ad you responded to," he snapped.

"I'm almost certain that cleaning was not in the job description," she said while she reached in her purse for the ad.

"If you've been in the childcare business for all these years you claim, then you will know there are numerous childcare duties that are expected from the nanny," John sneered. "These tasks should always come first and don't worry your pretty little head, darlin', I had my lawyer clearly express them in the contract you will be signing. If you can't fulfill these requirements, you won't be needed here."

"My God, what am I dealing with here," she replied under her breath through gritted teeth as she tried not to lose her temperament.

"I didn't catch that," John remarked.

"I will do everything you asked," she begrudgingly maintained. "But, only on one condition."

"I don't bargain with anyone," he chortled.

"Every great businessman always bargains as long as it is beneficial for him," she rebutted.

"Well, I am indeed prominent, but I could care less about anybody else's satisfaction. Either you do the job or the door is that way," he said as he pointed to the exit.

"Consider the job done, Mr. Monroe," Rachel stated with reluctance and a deep sigh.

"By the way, Mr. Monroe is my father's name," he corrected her. "Call me, John."

Chapter Eight

AFTER FILLING OUT all necessary paperwork for the job, Rachel settled into her room. Furious and with the need to vent, she immediately thought to call her father. Yet, she knew he was busy overseeing the family business, so she called her brother Michael, who was fiercely loyal and overprotective.

"Hey, congratulations! I heard the good news," He excitedly answered.

"Good news? Not so sure about that," she replied. "Ugh! I had no idea my first client would be a racist prick."

"Whoa! Calm down, angry woman," he tittered. "You know we don't talk like that. Remember, this is only temporary. Give it a few months. You know how important this is."

"Please talk to daddy, so I can come home. I don't want to work for this man," she pleaded.

"That's one big ask for this to be your first job," Michael chuckled. "Besides, you know how dad is."

"I know...I know," she sighed. "I haven't even started and I'm ready to come back home."

"Rachel stop stressing," Michael assured her.

"You know how to do this better than anyone. Now, my sweet sister is there anything else I can do for you?"

"Um yes, give me a new job," she humorously replied.

CHAPTER NINE

THE SUBSTITUTE TEACHER WAS APPROACH-ing fifty but the class of fourth-graders would say she looked close to one hundred. Some students would even go so far as to say that she looked like the artist Grandma Moses who they had recently learned about.

Whereas Mrs. Rose's voice was soft and invit-ing, the substitute's voice was loud and brash. Mrs. Rose would greet them in the morning while the substitute would hastily tell them to take their seats. To make things worse, she never gave them recess.

"Hand it over!" The substitute said as she stood over Sarah.

"But, Mrs. Rose always lets me keep my Tama-gotchis on my desk," Sarah whined.

"Do I look like Mrs. Rose?" The substitute questioned as her hands fell to her hips.

"No, Mrs. Rose doesn't look old like you, " Sarah replied.

The substitute did not know if Sarah intention-ally meant what she said or if her youth should be an excuse for such a rude comment. The laughter from the students swayed her opinion to that of

Sarah's comment was malicious and challenged her authority.

Without warning, the substitute snatched the toy out of her hand and locked it away in Mrs. Rose's desk. She also insisted that Sarah write her name on the chalkboard.

For most of the day, Sarah's face was stuck in a state of disbelief. Until art time, her lips remained as straight as the mechanical pencil on her desk. Crayola and RoseArt color pencils brought her out of her pouty mood.

Talented beyond her years, her work deserved to be on a canvas instead of white printer paper, but her innocent spirit did not care to know the difference.

"Check this out," She said to her deskmates as she held up the artwork.

The class complimented her as they laughed at the picture. Their giggles soon spread like wildfire and the substitute hopped out of her chair to see what the disruption was.

It appeared Sarah's desk had become a permanent stop for her. She stood mortified as she soaked in the children's cruel laughter. Her face twisted in disgust and reddened with anger as she snatched the artwork out of Sarah's hand.

During her twenty-five years as an educational professional, she had gotten picked on by children, but Sarah's caricature struck an untapped nerve. The drawing had a gargoyle effect on the substitute's nose and chin and her eyeballs bulged through eyeglasses. Sarah added further insult to injury by adding a speech balloon that read, "I'm the substitute and I'm a dodo head."

"Pack up your things young lady and go to the principal's office!" The substitute angrily said.

"What did I do?" Sarah complained.

"The better question is what didn't you do?" The substitute scolded. "You have been a troublemaker all day, and I have had it."

"But -" Sarah attempted to say.

"Be on your way, young lady," the substitute firmly said. "I will notify the front office to call your parents.

"Ooooooo," the class expressed in unison as she slowly packed her art box and trapper keeper in her Lisa Frank backpack.

"Maybe they can do a better job of disciplining you than I can," the substitute remarked.

CHAPTER TEN

THE GENTLE SCENT of gardenias kindled memories of a former life as John grabbed his blazer out of his bedroom closet.

Every week he had fresh flowers sent to Anna with a note that always said, "I count on your love to always brighten my day. I trust it always will. Up until this day, I have never been disappointed."

Nine years after her death, the flowers were still delivered weekly to his home.

Premature crow's feet deepened around his eyes as he smiled at a framed picture of his beloved wife. Her invisible presence was the only one who saw him smile. Though time pulled forward, he preferred to stay in the past and wanted no parts of anything that would threaten this arrangement.

Every day he wrestled with his memory as he fought not to lose the sound of Anna's voice or the touch of her skin. His fortune could never compare to the treasure of posed photographs and candid Polaroids he had of them together.

Their love always excited him, and he didn't care if they agreed or disagreed, fought or made love. No matter how extreme the contrast was, it was always worth his while because he was lucky to have Anna as his wife.

His silhouette of blackness casted a shadow on the frame as he allowed himself happiness. The sight of her engagement ring and wedding band sitting on their nightstand like props transported him back in time.

"So, John is it? Tell me, where do you see yourself in ten years?" Anna mocked her father while she and John held hands as they walked around her childhood neighborhood.

That was the question everyone who came into close contact with him asked as he approached college graduation. Most people did not know that the son of Bill Monroe was expected to join BetterLife Insurance, the family's business, the day he was born.

Bill founded the profitable business twenty-two years earlier. To continue family tradition, he sent John to the University of Mississippi to get a degree in finance. He wanted him to become an annuity broker and work his way up to president. He was proud that his son didn't have to face the uncertain job market that millions of graduates faced.

Even though John had wanted to take a year off and travel across Europe, he knew he could never say no to his father, who doted on him in public but practiced tough love at home. He never gushed over John's artistic talents as he was careful not to inflate his ego. He made deals, invested in real estate, and took care of his family. With John's entrance into manhood, he expected him to do the same thing.

"Babe, c'mon, you know where I see myself," John responded with agitation to Anna's teasing. "I've told you multiple times. Your dad has already interrogated me and I won't let you do the same."

It had been a long, hot, Mississippi night and John could not believe that his girlfriend had doubts about his future. From his viewpoint, this all stemmed from the conversation at Anna's father's birthday dinner.

From the moment they shook hands, her father, Jason, was not impressed. He joked that John's hands felt just as soft as his daughter's. In his opinion, John was a spoiled college punk from Atlanta who knew nothing about blue-collar hard work. He had no problem drilling John in front of her mom, kid sister, aunt and uncle about his choice to join his family's business.

"Annuities are too risky!" Jason squawked. "Especially in a recession."

He continued to make snide remarks at John throughout dinner. In his opinion, John was not good enough for his daughter and he wanted everyone to know.

Being the son of Bill Monroe, John was not accustomed to losing and stayed calm. He was game for whatever Jason wanted to play.

Always attentive, Anna could see John's frustration, which prompted her to suggest they take a walk under the Mississippi moon. She always knew what to do. A quality he valued in her.

"Someone is uptight. I was only kidding," Anna replied to John's comment about her acting like her father. "You've hurt my feelings. I can't believe that you think that way about me."

"I'm going to give you the world, babe," he stated with conviction.

At a sudden halt, she squeezed his hand to make him stop to face her. "That's the thing; you don't have to give me a rose garden. All I want is you, John Monroe. I know where you see yourself, so whatever my father believes doesn't matter because I have faith in you.'"

She gently placed her palm on his face, which soothed his soul. John took her hand and kissed it while he dropped to one knee. "Anna, will you marry me?"

His proposal left her speechless.

"I, um, I-I," John stuttered out of nervousness. "I know I don't have a ring, but I can get -"

"Yes! Yes! I will marry you!" Anna cut him off through her excitement, not caring about the lack of the ring.

That day was the milestone of a fresh beginning, or so he thought. The memory touched his heart like no other and made him glad he had chosen her for a wife. Strolls down memory lane brought tears to his eyes as he longed for her touch.

Even though Anna knew he was not a man of faith, she would often tell him, "God has us covered." The day she announced her pregnancy, it seemed like a dream as he exploded with joy. If he ever thought there was a God, it was at that moment.

Then, like a monsoon, everything was wiped away as a joyous event turned into the tragedy of his life.

"How could you build up a great life that I've always wanted to snatch away from me?" John screamed. "God has us covered?!? How!?!"

Unable to control his emotions, he slammed the picture on the dresser which caused the glass to shatter. He couldn't fathom why God would give him a wonderful woman only to take her away.

"John?" Rachel softly called out as her eyes glanced uncomfortably through his half-open bedroom door. She was empathetic at the site of a man ashamed to be vulnerable.

"Get out!!!" He fumed. He thought he had been crying in private and had not realized his bedroom door was cracked.

"But, it's about, Sarah," she gently urged. "I need to know what school she attends, so I can pick her up. The school just called saying she was disruptive in class."

A heavy silence settled over the house that created a weird tension.

"Woodruff Private Academy," he answered without looking in her direction as he still felt exposed.

"Thank you," she said as she carefully pulled the door shut.

CHAPTER ELEVEN

AFTER FINDING ENOUGH strength to make it out his house John headed to work. As he squeezed onto the elevator he shifted his tie when anxiety got the best of him. He did not feel comfortable around people, unless he was discussing a business deal.

"Hi, John! My name is Colin Cormick, and I started as a sales associate last week," the young man eagerly said. "I'm really looking forward to making an impact here."

Not one for small talk, John shook his hand and continued to look at the elevator door. He could not wait to get to his desk and send the office manager an email about the progress of the private elevator that was being built for him and his father. He disliked most of his employees and hated when they bombarded him with tedious questions.

"Good morning, John!" Paisley, his attractive assistant said. She wore a miniskirt to catch his attention as she greeted him at the elevator. "Mr. Monroe is very upset that you missed the 9 a.m. meeting and is demanding your whereabouts."

"What other meetings do I have today?" He

asked unbothered as he walked down the hall to his suite.

"Well, you are booked all day starting from now to seven this evening," she replied.

"Clear my schedule for the rest of the day and if anyone asks, tell them I'm not in the office," He instructed. "Also, I need some coffee, but none of that cheap stuff they have upstairs, so please go to Starbucks."

"Yes, sir," she said as she wrote everything down on a yellow note pad. "What do you want me to tell Mr. Monroe?"

"Tell him the sky is blue," he said with an attitude as he unlocked his office door.

"But what if-"

"Tell him, I'm not here, okay," he cut her off.

She attempted to follow him into the room, but the irritated look he shot her spoke volumes. Paisley got the hint and dismissed herself.

Within five minutes of placing his briefcase down on his desk, John's agitation reached new heights as his phone rang nonstop. Bill Monroe's name flashed over and over again across the phone screen.

He exhaled as he grabbed the phone handle. "Yes, dad."

"Paisley has informed me that you're sitting in your office even though I have a mandatory meeting penciled into your schedule!" Bill yelled. "There is money to be made, son."

"Paisley doesn't know how to follow simple instructions," John mumbled under his breath.

"What did you say?" Bill questioned.

"I NO LONGER NEED HER!" John screamed as he emphasized each word. "Paisley is fired."

"You can't terminate her for telling me the truth!" Bill shot back. "I hired that nice, beautiful, sweet girl. I won't allow it."

"Dad, I'm an equal stakeholder in this company and I can fire anyone that I please," John replied knowing it would get under his father's skin. "I don't need her or no one working here. My success comes from my hard work alone."

"Don't get above your raisin' son," Bill snapped. "You're making yourself out to be an arrogant prick. If your mama heard you talkin' like this, she would be ashamed. I am the founder of this company and it's only a success because of the people on payroll."

"Dad, you're the one who taught me how to spot a snake a mile away," John said with a sigh. "You should know better than anybody that just because a woman is attractive doesn't mean she's trustworthy. Clearly, she runs her mouth too much."

"Word of advice," Bill tiredly said. "Treat your employees like you would treat your customers so they keep coming back. Hopefully, you will realize this before you are left all alone in this world."

While on the phone, a picture of him and Anna caught his eyes, as his father's words reminded him of his reality.

"Haven't you noticed? I'm already alone, dad," John lowly said. "So are we done, now?"

Bill dropped the subject when he realized it was September, the month that Anna died. Every year around this time, John acted, more maddening than usual.

"We have a meeting at five. Be online ten minutes early because you're leading it," Bill said as he ended the call.

CHAPTER TWELVE

IMPULSES RARELY RULED John as he was a practical man, but with his hectic morning, he could not focus and yearned to clear his mind. He slipped out of the office without letting anyone know.

"If it isn't Johnny Boy!"Mack Barnes, his frat brother, yelled across the parking deck.

"Hey man! What are you doing?" John smiled surprised.

"We're supposed to be having lunch to celebrate my recent promotion and my hot new secretary. She's such a babe, man. She wears those really short skirts like Heather Locklear does on Melrose Place. I was just coming up to your office," Mack explained.

"Oh man, I'm sorry, I'm not gonna be able to make it," John apologized.

"Dude, c'mon. It isn't every day that your best bud becomes a partner at an ad agency," Mack disappointingly said. "Let's throw a few beers back at Two Pairs. You know they have the hottest waitresses in town."

"I'm not in the mood," John replied.

"Not in the mood? Mack questioned. "What

man with a pulse isn't in the mood to see beautiful women? We can bet on who can get the
most phone numbers like we did back in college.
Besides, you need to get your mojo back. You're
a single man, and it's time you start acting like it.
What do you think, Anna's gonna come kill you
from the grave if you move on?"

John glanced down at his white gold wedding
band, which he still wore on his ring finger.

"Buzz off man, you've gone too far," John said
as he walked away.

"Hold on, buddy!" Mack yelled as he trailed
after him. "You know what I mean! Anna was
like a sister to me! I just feel like you've been
in mourning for too long and it's time for you
to get back out there! Do you know how many
women ask me about my good pal, John Monroe?! You can have your pick at any bimbo in
Atlanta, dude!"

"Not interested," John said as he jumped over
his convertible Mercedes-Benz door.

"The John I met in college would be," Mack
pointed out.

"Bad comparison," John sarcastically laughed.
"We were kids. At forty, what kinda example are
you setting for your sons? No wonder why your
marriage was unsuccessful."

"And just who are you to judge me?" Mack
shot back.

"And just who are you to tell me I've mourned
my wife for too long," John fired back.

"Listen, man," Mack said to reconcile. "I didn't
mean to offend you, it's just people are thinking

you've gone koo-koo and as your friend, I feel it's my responsibility to make sure you ain't losing it."

"I can care less about what people have to say," John shrugged off the comment as he cranked his car. "Now if you'll excuse me, I have someplace to be."

CHAPTER THIRTEEN

IN THE SCHOOL'S front office, mesh stackable chairs were placed on top of dull grey carpet. A bulletin board contained thumb tacked school announcements and a painting of the building's namesake, Robert W. Woodruff, hung behind a woman who sat at an amber reception desk.

Even though Rachel had just walked in, the school's secretary looked angry. She donned short grey hair that was most likely styled in old-fashioned rollers. Her face was made up with discrete makeup except for her lips, which were cherry red and a blue Liz Claiborne cardigan dangled from her petite frame. The room was constantly being scanned by her small eyes.

"Hey, how are you doing? I'm here to pick up Sarah Monroe," Rachel said.

"Who are you?" The secretary asked with an attitude as she sipped Folgers coffee from a lipstick-stained mug that had a symbol of the school mascot.

Suddenly, it hit Rachel that she was probably not on the approved parent or guardian list. Since Sarah was a minor, there was no way the secretary would let her check-out the fourth-grader.

"I'm her new nanny. Matter of fact, this is my first day," Rachel rambled, hoping her explanation would sway the secretary's decision.

After a few more minutes went by, Rachel realized that she was getting nowhere with the secretary.

"Bless your heart. You've told me enough. It is against both school and county policy for me to release a student to any persons not on the approved list," she replied as her painted lips curved up in a sinister smirk.

Disappointed that she had not considered the stipulation, Rachel picked up her things and sauntered out of the front office. She trudged to the car in disappointment until it dawned on her to call John. She had hoped he would answer, but she became fed up after being forwarded to his voicemail three times.

She stormed back into the front office. "Look I understand you have your policies, but I am having a tough time contacting Mr. Monroe," she told the secretary. "I'm positive you know him, so you are aware of him being a complete pain in the -"

Before she completed her sentence a little girl with chestnut hair, braided in a fishtail, sat patiently and watched every word that came out of Rachel's mouth.

"Rear-end," Rachel finished her sentence, aware the little ears took notice. "I ask that you please do me this one favor until I can get on the list."

The secretary looked over her shoulder to

ensure no one was behind her. "I could not have described, you know who, more precisely," she laughed. "That little devil is a pain on my rump as well."

They both giggled, and Rachel felt relieved. "But," the secretary said as her brows arched. "I am sorry I just can't release her, ma'am."

Tension re-emerged on Rachel's face as she thought about quitting. This was more than she bargained for and certainly was not worth the strife.

"However," the secretary added after a sigh. "What I can do, is give those persons on the approved list a call to see if they will grant oral permission."

"Thank you," Rachel mouthed the words to the woman.

The secretary was not surprised when John did not answer the phone, so she gave a call to the second person on the list. '

"Hi Bill, this is Missy down at Woodruff Private Academy," she said. "I've been trying to get in contact with that son of yours, but I can't reach him. I've got a young lady up here at the school." She put her hand on the receiver and asked Rachel, "What did you say your name was again, hun?"

Rachel answered and the secretary continued her conversation with Bill. "Rachel says she's the new nanny and I wanted to make sure yall was alright with her bringing Sarah home."

Bill gave his consent and the secretary obliged by handing Rachel sign-out forms to complete.

"Are you going to call Sarah up?"Rachel asked.

"She is already up here," the secretary said with a Cheshire grin.

"Where?" Rachel asked.

The secretary pointed to the little girl with chestnut hair that had been sitting there the whole time.

"God, help me," Rachel said to herself as she walked toward Sarah.

"Hey, Sarah, I'm Rachel, your new Nanny. I'm going to be taking you home."

"Yeah, I figured that out like twenty minutes ago," Sarah replied with an eye roll.

"Oh, wow, wasn't prepared for that," Rachel mumbled to herself. "I definitely see the family resemblance."

"I wanna stop for custard before we get home,"the little girl demanded.

"No," Rachel declared as they walked outside. "Especially since you've used such a disrespect-ful tone. Besides, the schedule your father gave me includes nothing like that and besides, why should you be rewarded for such bad behavior?"

"It's not like my dad will punish me. He doesn't care about me. He never asks me about school or helps me with my homework. Next month we're having Donuts With Dad and everybody's daddy is coming except mine."

"Have you told your dad about it?"

"Every time I talk to my daddy he never lis-tens and even if he does, he never lets me finish talking." With a spot on imitation of John, she adds, "He cuts me off and says, 'I'm too busy.' She sighed, "He's always too busy."

Rachel's heart sank because she could not imagine her father never making time for her. No child should feel that way about their parents. She wondered if John was aware of how his behavior affected his daughter.

The rush hour traffic on Georgia 400 turned what was supposed to be a twenty-minute drive into one that was forty-five minutes. Through the window Sarah watched two school aged kids laugh and play in the mini-van in the next lane. She wished she had someone to relate to. Then maybe she would not feel alone.

Rachel glanced at her through the rearview mirror and saw unchecked tears flowing down her cheeks and dripping from her chin.

"My God, the spirit of this child is truly broken," she said to herself as she grew angry and wondered how John allowed his child to get to this emotional state.

"Do you listen to music, Sarah?" Rachel asked in a cheery manner.

"No," Sarah quickly replied as she hurried to wipe her face with her shirt sleeve. "My dad doesn't let me listen to music while in the car because he is always on business calls."

"Well, we are about to change that," Rachel said with a smile. "Let's see what we have here."

As Rachel scanned the radio channels, she asked, "What do you want to listen to? Rap? R&B? Jazz? Gospel?

"Ummmm, Britney Spears," she excitedly answered.

"Oh, so you're a pop girl," Rachel says with a slight chuckle. "Let's see if we can find Britney on the dial."

"You drive me craaaazy," Sarah sang as her eyes lit up. "That's my favorite song, and she's my favorite singer. I know all her dances because I record all her videos. I can show you when we get to my house."

"Look at you!" Rachel smiled. "I can't wait to see."

At this moment, Rachel realized regardless of the reason she scouted out John Monroe, her main mission was to now bring joy to Sarah's life.

"Do you want to go get ice cream?" Rachel kindly asked.

"But...I thought you said I couldn't."

"We'll find room for both," Rachel declared with a wink.

"But Daddy said…"

With a smile, Rachel completed her sentence, "Daddy will be OK. Trust me."

With a twist of the volume knob, they both sang to the top of their lungs, "You drive me craaaazy."

Traffic moved and finally, things seemed to be on the upside for both of them.

CHAPTER FOURTEEN

IT WAS LATE afternoon, John's heart pounded slow, but steady as he crept to the cold stone that was Anna's grave. He dreaded the cemetery, but he had to go there, better yet he needed to. He often wondered how someone among the living depended on the dead so much.

The gravestone was beautiful, polished, and smooth. All characteristics that Anna embodied when she was alive. Unlike his wife, it stood strong, erect, and would be there for at least a hundred years or more.

He kneeled down to read her name at eye level and ran his fingers over the engraved black lettering. The feel of the stone on his skin brought him peace as he laid down gardenias. Never in a million years did he think his last gifts for the love of his life would be a top of the line casket and gravestone. Still, this was the only place he felt he could talk to her and have it mean something more than just a memory.

"Hey Anna," he somberly said. "Today is the day. Our anniversary. Our wedding day was one of the most beautiful days of my life."

With his eyes shut and a smile on his face, he

continued, "You know, sometimes I can close my eyes and I can hear the music and see you dancing in your white wedding dress. Gosh, you were so beautiful. I can still see all the people throwing rice as they congratulated us."

Life with Anna was everything that he had imagined it would be. The day they took their marriage vows and said the words forever, he meant just that. Through sickness and health, till death did them part.

Their wedding day was one to be remembered. When he lifted her veil, she took his breath away. The green flecks in her eyes illuminated more than any day as he said the words, "I do."

"Agape," Anna whispered after they kissed.

It was a word she used to describe her love for him. It meant unconditional, and even in their worst, her love would remain undying.

"There is no me without you, so my love is eternal," John would always say.

Now he stood at her gravesite refreshing the flowers as he had done every week since her death.

"I –" he stopped and opened his eyes as though he were having a nightmare. "I know without a doubt, I'll never have a day like that again. Never."

"I'm so lonely," his voice cracked even though he tried to remain strong. "I've been thinking about you lately. As a matter of fact, I think of you all the time."

Unable to control his emotions, his eyes betrayed him and salty tears fell from his eyes irrepressibly. He could not form any words, so he patted his heart until he could manage to say, "You're always here."

He allowed himself more time to catch his breath before he started talking again, "I miss you so much, baby. Sometimes I get so frustrated because I can't reach you - wherever you are. I'd give anything...anything to see your beautiful face and hear your laughter again. I wish that you were here, so I could tell you about my day at night. I really miss our nightly chats."

At that moment, a birdsong came so sweetly, as the fall wind moved through John's hair. The naked trees had been deprived of color. Their precious leaves had fallen to the ground. John dried his eyes as he considered the scenery symbolic to his life with Anna. Like the tall trees he stood, and like the dry leaves her ravished body laid underground.

"Everybody keeps telling me to be happy and move on," he stated as he looked at her gravestone. "But how can I? It seems just like yesterday we were deciding on what we would name our baby...our child."

He looked downward and took a deep breath. "She needs you, Anna. Sometimes, I can't stand to look at her for too long because she reminds me so much of you. I don't understand why God took you away from me. I've never prayed harder than the day you died. I tried to make all kinds of bargains with God. But, still He took you!!"

"It's not fair!" He wailed. "It's not fair!!! How can I praise His name when He cut your life short?!How can I praise His name when He took you away from?! I can't."

The sound of a woodpecker caught his attention as he stood up to glance at his Rolex. It was 4:30pm, and he knew he had to leave, so he could prepare for his upcoming meeting.

"I will see you again one day, babe. I promise."

CHAPTER FIFTEEN

NURSERY RHYMES BLASTED from the out-door speakers at Cool Treats, a local ice cream parlor. It was the music that lured children to beg their parents for a cold sugary treat.

Once out of the car, Sarah skipped joyfully. She chased the merry tune all the way to the front door. Inside the restaurant, she and Rachel stood in line, jostling for positions to see the tubs of snacks.

"What kind of ice cream do you want?" Rachel asked.

"You mean custard," Sarah corrected her.

"Custard, ice cream, they're the same thing," Rachel commented.

"No, they're not," Sarah shot back in a bratty tone. "Custard is made with egg yolk and ice cream isn't. Duh!"

"Now wait a minute, little girl," Rachel sternly replied. "I won't allow you to talk to me like that. I've respected you since we've met and I expect the same thing from you. Do you understand?"

"Yes ma'am," Sarah promptly responded.

"I'm not that old," Rachel laughed. "Just call me, Rachel."

"Okay," Sarah smiled.

After sitting down at a table, Sarah grinned down at the bowl of desert, and ripped a plastic utensil out of its wrapper. She watched the custard until there was a golf ball sized lump in the middle and then stirred rapidly with her spoon. She never liked to eat the snack when it was so cold because according to her 'the flavor just didn't come through right.'

"Do you come here a lot with your father?" Rachel asked.

"My daddy only picks me up from school when he has too," she huffed. "He's not nice like most dads are to their kids. My Nana brings me here on the weekends."

Shock registered on Rachel's face and she tried to hide it with an awkward smile. "Why do you say that about your dad?" She questioned.

"Because either he's yelling at me or he's too busy with work," She explained. "We never do nothing fun.

Rachel had heard enough of Sarah's forlorn tales and did not want her dwelling on sad matters. "C'mon we better get going before your daddy wonders why we are not at home for dinner," Rachel urged as she got up to discard their things in the trash.

"He won't even notice," Sarah quipped.

Rachel was disgusted to learn that Sarah was being neglected. She thought children were treasures and the greatest gift a parent can give them was unconditional love. She had a bone to pick with John.

Chapter Sixteen

"WE NEED TO talk now!" Rachel demanded as she stormed into John's study oblivious that he was on a business conference call.

Struck by her boldness, John sat speechless as he tried to focus on two conversations that were not going well.

"Gentlemen, my apologies," he said through clenched teeth. "I have to drop because of a pressing issue that cannot wait."

There was tension in his manner and a tightness in his face, yet Rachel was unperturbed.

"What is it with you and closed doors?! Do you just like to invade people's privacy? Your pay is definitely getting docked for pulling a stunt like that," he threatened.

"Go ahead!" Rachel retorted. "I'm working this month free, anyway."

Every time she opened her mouth, he got angrier. Nobody had dared to speak to him in a manner he was concerned disrespectful. Especially, someone who was on his payroll.

"Tell me what is so vital that you forced me to get off a VERY important call? This had better be life or death," John demanded as he waited for answers.

His eyes wandered to a chair which he expected Rachel to take as an unsaid directive. The defiant spirit in Rachel would not allow her to sit. Until this point, she had danced on eggshells for John Monroe. Now, it was time to put her foot down and give him a piece of her mind.

She disliked his refusal to care about others. And she hated the way he walked around with an attitude as though he was mightier than everyone. His thoughts seemed geared only toward his own perceptions and feelings.

"Tell me, what could be so important that you purposely ignore my phone calls even though you know that if I'm calling it has to be something pertaining to your daughter?" She snapped. "I haven't even been here a full day, and I see how you neglect your child who adores you and craves your undivided attention."

Put off by her comments, John put his hand up to dismiss Rachel. He did not wish to engage in a conversation with a woman he regretted hiring.

"No! Answer the question," Rachel challenged as she grabbed his cordless phone, so he could not make a call.

"Woman, have you lost your everlasting mind!" John's temper flared as she put the phone behind her back.

"I'm perfectly sane and it's about time someone told you about yourself," she said as he chased her around the desk to get the phone back. "You need to be thrown in jail for child neglect and abandonment. Anything could have happened to your daughter, and you purposefully did not answer!"

"That's why I hired you!" He shot back.

"Oh, I get it," she said with a realization. "You hire a nanny to take your place. Feel all the emotions that you are supposed to. Act in all the ways that you as her father are supposed to. If it wasn't for the secretary knowing how much of a self-centered jerk you are, your daughter would still be at school. Do you even care about why the school called in the first place?"

"Oh, get off your soapbox!" He shouted. "Sarah is well taken of, and she has access to the finest things. All made possible because of my hard work."

"So, you're solely responsible for all your success?" Rachel asked.

"Of course!" John sarcastically responded. "My dad may have created the business, but I'm the brains and charisma that keeps it going."

"I-I-I! Me-me-me!" Rachel shouted as she shook her head out of disappointment. "Perhaps one day you'll realize that it's not all about you."

"Just what is that supposed to mean?" He questioned. "You know what, save it. If you ever pull a stunt like this again, you're outta here. Now, give me my phone."

"Sarah isn't the only thing you neglect," she sarcastically said. "Looks like you've been neglecting the gym as well. You're out of breath."

"Woman, you've got a lot of nerve," He chuckled.

"Dinner will be ready in an hour," she sorely

said as she walked to the door.

"Like hell, I'm not letting you cook dinner for me tonight," he said with a smirk. "My mama always said, "Son, when a woman cooks and she's upset with you she does strange things. And I ain't goin' for nothing strange. Order some pizza. Two medium pepperoni pineapple pizzas.'"

"Just when I didn't think the day could get any worse," Rachel laughed. "Pineapple on pizza? That has to be the worst topping combination ever."

"Here you go with your unsolicited opinions," John quipped with a smirk. "If you want to miss out on the glory and splendor that is pepperoni pineapple pizza. So be it. Order yourself something. But, I will gladly die on this heel defending the deliciousness that is pepperoni pineapple pizza."

This was the most animated Rachel had seen John in the few hours that she had known him.

"If only he was this passionate about Sarah," she thought.

CHAPTER SEVENTEEN

AFTER A YEAR of dating, John had proposed to Anna and they moved into a one-bedroom apartment together. They had difficulty at first. She was a clean freak and he was on the messy side.

Not to mention, they noticed the minor things about themselves that showed their upbringing. They argued over eggshells - a lot. Anna put them down the sink, and he preferred to throw them in the trash. They each thought how they were raised was the 'right' way. Eventually, they learned how to cohabitate.

On Valentine's Day, John laid in front of the TV, and waited for Anna to come home. Occasionally, he got up and moved the antenna when the television became fuzzy as he watched The Tonight Show Starring Johnny Carson.

Anna was disappointed that they couldn't spend the day together. She was still a first responder and worked long and unpredictable hours. John did not mind because he knew how much she loved her work. Plus, he loved the way she looked in her uniform.

John heard locks turn, and he smiled as he got

off the couch and saw his fiance holding a box.

"Happy Valentine's Day!" She said as she walked through the door.

"Babe, what's that?" He smiled.

"Our pie of love," she smirked.

"Oh, you shouldn't have," he joked.

"Anything for you," she said as he took the box and kissed her.

He smiled broadly as he opened the box of pepperoni pineapple pizza. Not only was he starving, but he couldn't resist sinking his teeth into a slice. When he offered Anna a slice, she laughed and tried to resist taking a bite, but John kept urging her to "open up."

"It's so gross," she giggled as she chewed a bite.

"But, you love me regardless," He beamed as he kissed her.

"That's right! And don't you ever forget it," she replied.

Chapter Eighteen

JOHN HAD A bittersweet smile as he looked at an open box of uneaten pepperoni pineapple pizza that sat on his desk. He could not muster up the strength to eat a bite on their special day.

"So romantic. So dumb. So cute." He thought. "Now those days are gone. Just like the dreams of the future I had for Anna and me."

An unusual sound filled the house and sent John out of his thoughts and out of his study.

"What's going on here?!" John demanded as he barged into the den. His eyes quickly scanned the room and spotted an open pizza box, construction paper, glitter and other art supplies he considered clutter.

"We were playing paper-scissor-rock for the last slice of pepperoni pineapple pizza, and Rachel won the last slice. She won't share any with me," Sarah laughed.

"Hahaha, I so underestimated this pizza!" Rachel commented. "It is really good."

"I used to think it was gross too," Sarah smiled. "But, my dad loves it so much."

Even though a few of her teeth were missing, she looked just like her mother. Her giggle prompted John's memory to a time when the arrival of her birth was all he and Anna talked about.

"Babe, which dress do you like best?" Anna asked as she repetitively alternated two dresses in front of her.

"Babe, please don't kick me out of our comfortable bed, but those look a bit small," John chuckled as he adjusted the pillows underneath his head.

"So, you have jokes, huh?" She smiled and threw a decorative pillow at him.

"Just saying," he laughed as he caught the pillow. "In case you haven't noticed, your belly is protruding.

"I know," she whined as she looked in a full length wall mirror. "I've been sharing my body with our little girl for eight months, but the moment she's here, I'm hitting the gym. Mama's gotta get her figure back."

John got out of bed and walked over to his wife. "And how are you so certain it's a girl?" He asked as he grabbed her waist and kissed her on the lips.

"Because I just have a feeling," she coyly said in between kisses.

"My two girls," he smiled and put his hand on her belly.

After basking in his embrace, she turned around. "So, which one do you like?"

"Hahahaha, you're still stuck on this?"

"Yes," she playfully answered. "I have to plan what I will wear when you take me out after having the baby."

"Either, babe," John replied. "You look good in anything."

"Nobody makes a corny line sound more believable than you," she giggled.

"Well, no woman makes being indecisive about her wardrobe sexy like you do," he smiled before kissing her.

If Sarah had not called his name repeatedly, he would have stayed down memory lane. Out of his past and back in the present he was even more upset than he was before.

"Clean up this mess, now!" he demanded.

"But, daddy, I was only -" Sarah excitedly said as her cupid bow lips stretched into a smile that did not quite reach her sad eyes.

The forced expression made Rachel's heart heavy. For a few moments, she stared at John from the couch, and hoped his expression would mirror his daughter's. But it never did, and it broke her heart.

"I don't want to hear it!" He yelled. "Clean this up and go to bed!"

The loudness in his voice caused Sarah to flinch and tears filled her eyes. She tried her best to hold it in out of fear her father would become more agitated if he saw she was crying.

As Rachel sat and observed, her thoughts

gnarled together and a strong desire to say something to John about his behavior towards Sarah.
One look at Sarah and she had enough. "Hey,
that's no way to treat your daughter," she said as
she caught up with him in the hallway.

"And that's no way to treat my home," he shot
back. "I'm paying you to look after my daughter.
Not to act like a freakin' child."

"Maybe if you adopted a more childlike attitude, you could bond with your daughter," she
commented. "I haven't known that little girl for
a full twenty-four hours and I know her better
than you do!"

"And what's that supposed to mean? Sarah is a
happy little girl with the gift of gab. Of course,
she is going to talk to you!" John shot back.

"Your daughter smiles because she is a child. It
is the way of children," Rachel explained. "She is
full of pain and hurt from the way you treat her.
Just a few minutes ago, she tried showing you a
picture she drew especially for you, but you just
blew her off! It is your responsibility as a parent to give Sarah your approval and show her the
patience and reliable love she needs. A child can
only show their real selves if a safe space is created
for them. She may giggle, but she is hiding her
real emotions underneath. A child can't merely
be accepted; they have to feel wanted. Mark my
words, the older she grows the more she will start
to rebel due to the lack of love she receives from
you right now."

"It must be that time of the month? Don't you
think you're being a tad bit dramatic?" He sarcas-

tically quipped.

"If that isn't the most sexist thing!" Rachel shouted in outrage. "You tell me which is worse: a woman on her natural monthly cycle or a man with a life long inflated ego?"

"Just who do you think you are to tell me about my child?!" He questioned in outrage.

"If nobody has ever told you, I will. You're emotionally and physically numb to your child," she said.

A string of curse words flew out of his mouth as he snapped. "You know nothing about my life. Stop trying to be a shrink and pack your bags. You can stay the night, but you won't be needed tomorrow or thereafter."

CHAPTER NINETEEN

RACHEL WAS STUNNED to find a spotless room when she returned to the den.

"You sure do clean fast," Rachel said as she tried to conceal the disappointment in losing her job.

"When daddy yells like that, he's really mad," Sarah sadly said. "Sometimes I think he doesn't love me."

"How often does he lose his temper?" Rachel asked as her concern grew.

"Not much," she answered as she wiped the last bit of glitter off the table. "Sometimes he just gets in bad moods."

Rachel continued to question John's behavior, but stopped after Sarah's answer became shrugs.

"Wow, this is really good," Rachel said as she picked up Sarah's drawing. "Who do you get your drawing skills from?"

"I dunno," Sarah replied. "I just know that everyone likes my work. Everyone except the stupid substitute."

"Sarah, it's not nice to talk about your teacher that way," Rachel nicely scolded.

"She's not my teacher," Sarah corrected. "Mrs. Rose cares about me. The substitute is just a mean old lady who I hate. She just wants to get me in trouble."

"Hate is a strong word," Rachel lectured. "The substitute was only doing her job which isn't easy. Art is powerful and should inspire, not make people feel crappy. Don't you want everyone to feel warm and fuzzy inside when they look at your work."

"Yes, ma'am," Sarah nodded.

"Hey, what did I tell you about this ma'am business," Rachel laughed.

"I mean Rachel," Sarah smiled.

"That's better," Rachel commented.

"But everyone thought it was funny," Sarah replied.

"Just like your father you have to have the last word, huh?" Rachel quizzically remarked. "Everyone might have thought it was funny, but it made the substitute feel sad. You don't wanna be a mean girl, do you? I'm sure your parents don't want you acting that way."

More than ever, Sarah wished she had a mom to talk to. "Daddy would be mad if he found out I was still down here. Goodnight."

"Do you want me to tuck you in?" Rachel asked.

"Nobody has tucked me in since pre-school," Sarah replied as she headed for the stairs.

CHAPTER TWENTY

SARAH'S DISPOSITION LINGERED IN RACHEL'S mind. It was all too much for her to bear. The moment she knew Sarah was upstairs, she called her father.

"Hey, my precious one," her father joyously said.

"Hey daddy," she said. "I just needed to hear your voice."

When her father asked if everything was okay, Rachel's voice cracked as she explained how she had been fired.

"Even though I can't stand this man, I still didn't want to be fired," she stated.

"Don't cry. Everything will be alright," her father assured.

"Maybe I should have kept my mouth shut," she remarked. "But, you've always taught me to stand up for what I believe in. The way he interacts with his daughter breaks my heart. A father can scare a child for life with distance."

"Yes, that's true," her father agreed. " Did you ever think that there is pain behind his shouts?"

"Even if it is, that doesn't make the way he talks to people right, daddy," she rationalized. "I just feel so sorry for this little girl because she's helpless in the situation. I can't imagine not growing up with your active presence. Even today, I still need to receive your positive affirmations. The man doesn't seem to have a loving bone in his body. When I called him out for his lack of affection, he blew up and told me to be gone by morning."

"Well, you certainly won't be the first person in our family who has been underestimated," he commented.

"Can you believe that she feels her teacher loves her more than her father? I want to bring her home, daddy. The other children will love her," she pleaded.

After a brief silence, he replied, "Sweetheart, you know the timing is wrong. And that is not your objective for being there."

"I know," she answered, defeated.

"One thing is for certain, that little girl will never forget the kindness you showed her today," he mentioned. "Your good works will continue on."

"You really think so, daddy?"

"I'm confident that everything will work itself out," he said. "This is a very important client, so why don't you attempt to get your job back?"

"Daddy, I'm not about to beg that man," she said.

"Who said anything about begging? I'm merely suggesting that you talk to him and see if he'll understand your logic since you've both calmed down. Seek first to understand before understood."

"Um, I'll think about it daddy."

"I have a feeling that he will come around eventually," he noted.

"For Sarah's sake I hope so," she responded.

"Look, don't worry. I love you. Your brother is calling, let me see what he wants."

"OK, daddy, I love you."

Chapter Twenty-One

SOFT WATER DROPLETS hit the car window as John drove down the street with a vengeance, as though he had another body at home. His foot tapped the gas pedal as his ZR1 Corvette fast approached the back of a Dodge Ram, which he often referred to as a pollution belcher. With no fear, he zoomed around the truck.

Russian roulette was not a game he was afraid to play. The higher the speed rose on his speed-ometer, the more his temper climbed as he thought about Rachel. He couldn't believe that she was disrespectful enough to insult his parent-ing skills. There were ten other nanny applicants that he wished he had hired. But, now he was desperate and had to put up with a disruptive employee. Tomorrow she would be gone, and nothing would change that.

'Every Rose Has its Thorn' by 1980s hair band, Poison, played on the radio. John could not believe his ears. It was Anna's favorite song. No matter what he did, everything around him seemed to trigger Anna. The present moment was never as sweet as his memories.

All he wanted was a peace of mind. It was only one place where he could get that – his office.

CHAPTER TWENTY-TWO

DONE WITH CLEANING the house, Rachel debated on if she should approach John about the incident in the hallway. She looked at the digital clock and saw that it was 8:30 pm.

Naturally, she walked to the last place she saw him go - his bedroom. Gently, she walked up the stairs to find his bedroom door open. The room was beige with beautiful murals on the wall, hand painted by a professional. Her bad nerves became frayed as she knocked on the open door and called his name, which he did not answer.

Next, she headed to his study with the thought that he must have slipped in there when she was on the phone with her father. An open pizza box sat on his desk with all twelve slices intact. To her surprise, he was not there either.

Perhaps he had gotten a taste for something else and was in the kitchen fixing a snack. The stainless steel refrigerator door was closed and bare of kid drawings and magnets. The pantry was closed as well. He wasn't there either.

On a second unofficial tour of the house, Rachel passed the dining room. It was a grand space, to say the least. There was no television, no bookshelf, no dining table, only the chairs arranged around the bespoke fireplace which leaped with a gas flame. More importantly, there was no John Monroe.

CHAPTER TWENTY-THREE

JOHN RELISHED THE opportunity to soak in his thoughts without disturbance. The moon reflected off the glass windows of the Monroe owned tower as he parked his car for the valet. At their old and much smaller office, he would love when he worked late hours and Anna would unexpectedly beam up to his office for a late-night dinner.

Tonight, dinner would be take-out from the China Cafeteria. The taste of sesame chicken and shrimp fried rice bounced off his taste buds as he placed his order over the phone. His minibar had emergency rations of four full bottles of gin and whiskey. He twisted open the cap and took a big gulp.

"Babe, we had it all worked out. The life we dreamt of," John stated in utter sadness as he stared at a black and white portrait of Anna that sat on his desk. "Everything had fallen into place. We were so much in love we couldn't see straight. I'd never been happier. Our future seemed so bright."

Plane tickets left on his desk by his ex-assistant, Paisley, for an upcoming business trip jogged his memory back to Anna's first trip to Atlanta. She was so nervous about getting on a plane for the first time that she held his arm the whole flight.

"Anna, you're gonna cut off my circulation," he laughed as she clutched his arm. "Relax babe, the turbulence is over."

"Are you implying that this airplane is turning me into a scaredy cat?" she joked.

"Yeah, pretty much," he laughed. "But, if that's what keeps you close to me, my arm is at your service."

"It better be," she said before kissing him.

" I can't wait until you see my family home and meet my folks. My mama says she feels as though she knows you already because every time I phone home I'm talking about you," he beamed with pride.

"I'm just so nervous," she joyfully screamed.

"Don't be babe," he heartened as he kissed her hand. "You're the daughter my parents never had."

John stewed over his thoughts. "I guess it was all too good to be true. I would have never thought in a million years it would end this way. Here's to us!"

As he finished off a bottle of Cambridge gin, the extension buzzer went off like an annoyed rattlesnake. The last thing he wanted to do was talk to anyone. A number with a 770 area code flashed on the screen. Over and over Rachel called, but John opted to take a shower and change into something more comfortable before he picked up his food order.

In between Rachel's call, Bill also phoned to find out why John had dropped the conference earlier in the evening. After several attempts, he left a scathing message reprimanding his son about the importance of staying on a business call for it's scheduled duration.

The hot shower opened up John's pores and washed off the day's grime, but it did not remove the melancholy that seeped in his spirit.

While the night continued to roll over as the storm shower ceased, he eventually got dressed in jeans and a t-shirt. An everyday task that would normally take him no more than five minutes to complete took twenty minutes. The consumption of two bottles of alcohol had left him uncoordinated.

Once he made it down the elevator he smoothly stumbled across the lobby. Still having some wits about him, he popped a few Tic-Tacs in his mouth before he headed to the sidewalk. He waited patiently near a lamp post that had an orange-yellow glow.

"Hello," a dark-haired woman who waited on a cab nicely said.

"Hello?" John questioned with an attitude. "Why are you putting on a mask of false friendliness just to say hello to a man you don't know or care about?"

"Maybe I want to get to know you better," she winked. "Just showing a little southern hospitality. Besides, being nice to an attractive man is never a hard act of kindness."

"When did 'hello' become so insignificant?" John ranted as he ignored the woman's flirtation even though he was not oblivious to it. "No one bothers to say anything of meaning anymore. Tell me when did saying 'hello' become a tool in our pointless existence?"

Under sober circumstances, John would have not felt a burning desire to be brutally honest, but with no control to filter himself, muddled words continued to pour out of his mouth.

"Here comes my cab now," the woman politely said. "You don't seem to be in any condition to drive. Wanna share with me?"

"Ha! And just what is that supposed to mean?" He bitterly laughed. "A man can't even express how he feels without being called a drunk."

"It's your choice," the woman said with a seductive smile as she climbed into the cab. "The night is still young."

"I'm good, sweetheart," John said as he closed the cab door and waited for the valet to bring his car.

CHAPTER TWENTY-FOUR

THE CHINA CAFETERIA was one exit away as John sped down the freeway. Bill Monroe was the last thing on his mind, yet he could not continue to refuse his calls.

"Yes, father," John slyly answered. "What do I owe the honor?"

"Well, I see someone's got some liquid courage in him," Bill gruffed.

His son's drunken tone offended him. This behavior was becoming the usual and he hated it. Weakness or grief were emotions he couldn't understand.

John could not figure out his father's tough demeanor. He once asked his mother why Bill was so cold. She replied that growing up during the great depression left him psychologically scarred.

In the Black Belt of the South, things had gotten so bad for Bill and his family on their small farm, that at eleven years old, he took three years off from school due to a drought which began in 1930.

They had an insufficient irrigation system and their soil was depleted, all of which made their cash crops worthless. Also, during this period his mother was pregnant with twin boys, Taylor and Baylor, who were malnourished at birth due to the family's inadequate diet that consisted mainly of molasses, fatback, and cornbread. The twins only lived for a week before they died of complications. With not even a dime to spare, his father, a prideful man, buried the infants in two size twelve JC Penney's shoeboxes. Two years later, his mother would succumb to pellagra. Very early on, tragedy had made acquaintances with Bill.

"Son, I've never claimed to be Einstein, but it ain't a good idea for you to be behind the wheel," he warned.

"Aw, c'mon dad, me and the boys used to throw back way more than this in high school and you had no problem with it," John countered.

"Times were different," Bill snapped. "The only thing that hasn't changed is you still think you're living for yourself."

"Just what does that supposed to mean?" John questioned.

"Listen, you're not ready to hear that truth," Bill cautioned. "And that ain't the reason I'm calling. You hung up on one of our biggest clients, John, and they are pissed! What in the devil has gotten into you, boy?:

"You mean to tell me the founder couldn't smooth things over?" John said sarcastically. "I had an emergency."

"What was so important, John?!"

"I do have a daughter."

"Since when have you shown Sarah any attention?"

Barely unable to keep his focus as he got off the highway, John became incensed. "What do you mean?!? I do show her attention, I'm just busy!"

"That's just the excuse you keep using John, and you know it!"

The tires hissed over the newly poured black pavement as John shouted into the phone. "Don't tell me how to raise my daughter!! I don't recall you winning any father of the year awards when I was growing up."

"You're right. I haven't been the best dad to you," John admitted. "But, you had your mama to nurture you. Sarah's a motherless little girl in need of a loving parent. There's only so much your mama can do now. When are you going to be a stand-up man and give her the love and attention she deserves? Busy is just an excuse and I'm not going to let you keep using it. The same time you're devoting to drinking, and sulking could be spent with Sarah. John, all I'm saying is don't make the same mistakes I've made. Sarah longs for your recognition and if you don't give it to her soon, she will seek it elsewhere."

"Not you too!" John whined. "She's fine dad and if this is all you're gonna talk about, then I must go."

"Anna's heart would break if she saw you right now," Bill commented.

"Don't you dare bring her name up!" John screamed as his eyes brimmed with tears. "You have no right!"

"Son, you need closure!" Bill yelled. "Only

God can give you that."

"God!!! God!!! You tell him the only closure I will ever get is if he gives me back my wife," John said before he closed his flip phone and threw it on the passenger seat.

As he got off the highway exit, he took his rage out on the road. It was a two-lane street, and the Porsche that rode in front of him was his new enemy. John attempted to go around the car, but headlights from an approaching car in the next lane blinded him. In an instant, he lost the opportunity to evade an abandoned broken-down BMW.

The Corvette flipped and took out the BMW and itself. Both cars spun. John could barely scream before the airbags knocked him back and sideways. The seat belt snapped, and he launched forward breaking the windshield. His ejected body laid feet away from the vehicle on a dark road.

Chapter Twenty-Five

"JOHN. JOHN. JOHN." A soft voice woke him up.

His brain stuttered for a moment while his mouth tried to catch up with his thoughts. He laid speechless at the sight of a woman with voluminous golden hair that draped her ivory shoulders.

"Anna?" He confusingly questioned as he was unsure if he was hallucinating.

He held his breath, hoping it was not a dream as he stood to close the distance between him in the room. When his eyes met her green eyes, he knew. He stood speechless. Anna was a perfect picture of time without hands or measure. She had not aged a single year.

"What are you doing, John?" She asked with a crumpled face as she took a step back.

"Anna, babe, please tell me this is real," he begged as he stood paralyzed.

"It is," she replied as a halo of light surrounded her whole body.

"I've missed you so much," he cried.

"Our beautiful baby girl is longing for your love, but you don't see that," she responded.

"You only came back to judge me?!" He yelled in disappointment. His frustration grew as he was powerless to stop the tears that rolled from his cheek. "You left me! You left me to raise a daughter that I have no guide for. I don't know how to be a parent."

His defensive tone did not change her serenity. "John, you don't need a guide to love."

"You were my guide!" John exclaimed. "I need you, Anna!" he pleaded. "We were supposed to be great! God took that away from me. How will I ever love again? You are the love of my life."

A tear rolled from her eye. "God didn't take that away from you. If you would open your eyes, you would see that my love has remained right in front of you. I left you with a part of me, John!"

More tears poured from both their eyes as every stride he took forward, she took a step backward.

"I chose you as my husband for a reason, but every day that passes you fail me."

Ashamed by her statement, he lowered his gaze. "But I still believe in you," she continued. "I know you are in pain. That's why I'm here now."

His eyes drooped as he commented, "I don't understand. Why show up now?"

"Because I want you to understand you are not the only person who hurts. Sarah has cried out for nine years and I have heard her cry. I couldn't bear it any longer," she explained.

"What about my cry?!" He screamed in outrage. "Have you ever thought about that or even heard it?! Everyone keeps saying the same thing Anna, but trust me no one feels my pain!"

"John, you know I would never intentionally leave you," she rationalized.

"I just feel you gave up on me, babe," he revealed. "One minute you're with me and the next you're gone. If only you had listened to me and did things the traditional way."

"It was predestined, John, and uncontrollable," Anna resolved. "You can't keep blaming me or yourself. There was nothing I could do."

"Well, why won't you let me hug you?" John questioned. "Every night I wish I could hold you tight. Every morning I wish I could kiss your sweet lips. I'm here with you now, so why won't you let me embrace you?"

"My love is refraining me from touching you, John," she said. "God knows I want to be hand in hand with you and our little girl."

"Then come to me, baby," he urged. "I'm begging you please come back home."

Anna's lips trembled and her voice cracked as she spoke. "If I come, you will have to stay."

"Okay. What's wrong with that?" He responded. "For ten years, I've been longing for your touch! I will give everything up just to feel you in my arms again."

"John, listen to me," she pleaded. "If we embraced, it can only last a moment."

"Why?! Why only for such a brief time?" He asked.

She let out a lengthy sigh as her eyes narrowed. "Your heart isn't right with God. You've strayed so far from Him. He loves you, John. So, He has allowed me to speak with you amongst other reasons."

Her statement baffled John and for a minute he stood there confused. "What does that mean? Other reasons like what?"

"I'm here to show you the pain you are causing our child."

Lights swirled, and instantly he and Anna hovered over his mansion. A streak of light focused on the inside of his house. From heaven, they saw little feet sliding across the hardwood floor in an ill-fated attempt of trying to be silent.

"Daddy, told me to go to bed, but I want you to braid my hair," the tiny voice said.

"Sure," Rachel replied as Sarah plopped on the couch.

"Who styled your hair in fish tails this morning?" Rachel questioned.

"The old nanny. Those braids were like three days old," Sarah explained.

"Well, I couldn't tell," Rachel responded.

"Can I ask you a question?" Sarah curiously said.

"Of course," Rachel acknowledged.

"Do you think my daddy loves me?" Sarah shyly asked.

"Yes," Rachel answered cautiously because of her opinions of John's parenting skills.

"But, he doesn't show it like other dads," she cried. "He never tucks me in at night and he almost never ever gives me hugs and kisses."

Rachel tried to find words to soothe her as she continued braiding her hair. "Your father loves you, but sometimes parents may not always show it because they have so many things to deal with."

"But he never shows it," Sarah shed more tears.

"That's because he doesn't know how. Your mother was everything to your father and when she died, I think the joy he had inside him died too," Rachel mindfully said.

"And he blames me," Sarah sadly said.

Rachel wanted to kick herself for making matters worse. "No baby, he doesn't blame you. He faults himself. Your daddy loves you. One day he will let you know how special you are. He will come around, trust me."

"I don't think so," Sarah complained as she wiped her eyes.

"My darling, never forget, love conquers all. You will see," Rachel replied as she kissed Sarah on the forehead. "Your mother is watching over you and God loves you."

Sarah grinned as Rachel embraced her the way she wished both of her parents could every day.

"I like talking to you," Sarah responded with a smile. "Tomorrow after school, can we stop by Cool Treats again?"

"Well," Rachel hesitantly maintained. "We'll have to see what tomorrow brings."

"That means yes," Sarah smiled wide enough to reveal missing teeth.

"All finished! How do you like it?" Rachel asked once she weaved the last hair strand.

"I love it!" Sarah beamed.

"And to think your father thought I couldn't do your hair," Rachel joked.

"Pinkie promise you won't tell daddy I got out

of bed," Sarah requested as she lifted her small finger.

"Pinkie promise," Rachel said as she wrapped her fifth finger around Sarah's.

A wave of emotion hit John from above which caused him to weep as he fell to his knees. In that moment, he gained a newfound respect for Rachel. Never once did she speak ill about him when she gave Sarah her best explanation of his behavior towards her.

"This is not the first night that Sarah has cried over you," Anna informed him as they levitated away from the view. "I've waited to visit you because I had faith that your mourning would pass."

"The hurt won't go away!" He cried

"John, God can take the pain away. But, you have to open your heart to Him. I know that our love is eternal and we will be together one day."

"But, not today, huh?" He questioned.

"John, our baby needs you," she replied in that sweet tone and all too familiar smile.

This was the first time she had smiled since their celestial reunion. Within minutes he was transformed into the college kid she had met that fateful night many years ago.

"I love you so much, babe," he stated with every breath in his body. "If I can't stay here with you, please come back with me. Please. I don't want to leave you up here alone."

"You don't understand," Anna said as her head dropped.

"No, Anna, frankly I don't," John replied with

a frown.

"I've tried telling you, but your heart is not allowing you to receive the message," she patiently explained. "Before I understood my situation, I made appeals to God to come back to you and Sarah. But, I can never be a part of the Earthly world. What we shared will live in your memory forever and will always be suspended in time."

"But, I need your love...I need you," John begged.

"My aura is invariably with you even in your darkest hour," she explained as a single tear fell from her eye. "I want you to remember that there is a love greater than mine that lives in you. God's love saved me and is the reason why I am here today. You are never alone, John, because He is always with you. Do right by our daughter. She needs an active, attentive father. Worldly possessions are not enough. As you see, they mean nothing here."

John looked around and saw endless white velvet clouds and understood what she meant.

"Don't be afraid to allow yourself to love again," she continued.

"Love again!?" John shouted. "I could never love a woman the way I love you."

"I know," Anna assured him. "All I'm saying is have an open heart to the idea."

"You're the one I love, Anna," John stressed.

"I love you eternally and everlasting. Free your heart for love. I will see you again."

Suddenly, his eyes turned raw and blind and a warmth weighed on his chest.

CHAPTER TWENTY-SIX

THE LAST THING on Rachel's mind was following the plot of a show or laughing with a laugh track as she packed her suitcases. She dreaded leaving Sarah.

Above the mantle in her guest room hung a painting that held her eyes. "It's too small," she thought.

The brush strokes were tiny and controlled. She did not know much about art, but something about this piece of work was off. The question that stood at the forefront of her brain was whether or not it was incomplete or was it intended to look this odd.

Teeth. Teeth. Teeth. They were straight. They were perfect. Yet, realistically defined. A smile without a face. Peculiar. Even though the composition was plain and simple it dominated the wall. Both stunning and head-ache inducing. Like a novel condensed into a single page. Rachel wanted to know the backstory. The inspiration.

"Who would leave this picture unfinished and let alone sell it?" She said aloud. "Why would John buy this?"

Rachel stepped closer to examine the signature.

"J. M. Could it be...John?"

She walked around the house and examined other portraits that hung from the wall and they all had the same signature.

"Wow, so this is where Sarah gets it and she doesn't even know it." Rachel shook her head as the rung. She ran downstairs and answered the phone in the den.

"Hello, is this the nanny?"

"Yes, this is Rachel speaking."

"Hi Rachel, I'm Bill Monroe. Sarah's grandfather and John's father. I'm gonna need you to bring her down to Northside hospital," he informed.

"Why? What's going on?" She panicked.

"John's been in a bad accident...things aren't looking too good."

CHAPTER TWENTY-SEVEN

MOST CHILDREN LEARNED about death when their first goldfish died, but Sarah was different. At two, she found out her mom lived in heaven Now, she repeatedly asked God not to take her dad to live in the sky with the mother she never met. The grim reality of her daddy dying brought about flashes of the redhead Orphan Annie in her mind. She wondered if she would end up in a similar circumstance if her dad did not make it.

Rachel silently prayed as she never would have imagined she would be in this predicament. "Father God, I ask that you keep your hand over this family. I know they aren't the closest, but perhaps if you let John live through this potential tragedy this will change the trajectory of their lives."

She needed to stretch her limbs after hours of sitting in Northside Hospital's waiting room. "Anybody want a soda?" She asked the family as she got up from the maroon-cushioned seat.

"No, thanks, we're fine," John's mother dryly responded.

"Um, I'll take a Pepsi," Sarah quickly replied as

her legs dangled from the chair.

"Pepsi? Are you sure? You're from Georgia, the land where Coca-Cola originated," Rachel lightly joked, which made many of the distressed family's laugh.

"That's her mama's blood in her," Bill chuckled.

Sarah hated when people made remarks like her grandfather did. It made her sad and to a certain extent jealous because someone else knew her mom. A person who had remained a mystery to her. Tons of questions always filled her head. How did she sound? What made her laugh? What was her favorite color? Did she love her?

As she waited for Rachel to bring her soft drink, the fourth-grader realized she often had similar questions about her daddy, too. She panicked as she thought about the possibility of never being able to get those questions answered.

A stoic nurse entered the waiting room in blue scrubs and walked over to the Monroe family. She patted her pockets and let out a slow breath. "We've done all we could."

"What!?!" Bill shouted as his hands shook uncontrollably.

"The doctor has asked for the family to come into the room."

CHAPTER TWENTY-EIGHT

HOURS PASSED.

Bill and his wife had gone home to get some rest because John's status had not changed. When they offered to take Sarah home with them, she was adamant about staying at the hospital with her daddy.

Rachel drifted off to sleep twice as they sat in the room, but Sarah stayed awake through the wee hours of the morning. To help curve her tiredness, Rachel got coffee and breakfast for them both at the hospital's cafeteria.

John awakened to the sound of a heart monitor, IV's, and oxygen tanks attached to him. Slowly, his swollen eyes pried open to meet a dismal view of fluorescent lights. His eyes took some time to adjust as his breaths matched the beeping of the machines that surrounded the bed.

"Daddy! Daddy!" Sarah's screams of excitement startled him. "Daddy's awake! Daddy's awake!" She ran out of the room to alert the nurses.

Even though John had been distant and ignored her for most of her life, his daughter was by his side. He was deeply touched.

The tubes in his mouth left him unable to

speak, but his exasperated hums grabbed every-one's attention once they resurfaced in the room. Rachel nearly crushed the styrofoam containers that held their breakfast with her fingers out of shock.

Sarah walked over to her father as she could not believe God granted her wish. Once she was close enough, John reached for her hand. Remorse and apology filled his eyes as he attempted to speak.

"Sssh! Don't speak," Rachel replied.

The nurses took his vitals as they spoke a for-eign medical language to John. Gratitude was the only thing he understood because he was lucky to be alive.

After the nurses confirmed that John was stable they left the room. One of them left their writ-ing pad down and pen on the over-bed table and John grabbed it. He wrote and held up, 'WHY AM I HERE?' Any adult would have mistaken his large handwriting for that of his daughter's.

"You were in a serious car accident and suffered a concussion and a broken leg, to say the least," Rachel explained. "But the nurses and police say that you were supposed to have died. The impact of the windshield should've killed you. Your body was thrown twenty feet. This is miraculous!"

John rubbed his hand against his lumpy fore-head. He tried to recall the events that led to this, but his mind was jumbled with too much chaos. Especially flashes of him with Anna, which led to confusion. The memories were too vivid for something that happened ten years ago.

"I'm not shocked. I told them you are special

and God loves you," Rachel continued with a wink. "Since your life wasn't taken in the crash, then God has more for you to do. What do you think?"

John looked at Sarah's innocent face, full of hope and nodded. He closed his eyes and gripped his daughter's hand firmly. A gesture she had yearned for all of her life. She beamed with pride and could not stop smiling.

"I love you, daddy."

For the first time he truly heard his daughter. If there was anytime he wished he could talk, it was then. He owed his daughter more than she ever knew. Through the soreness of his muscles, he picked up the nurse's pad and wrote the words Sarah dreamed of hearing. 'I love you too, princess. I'm so sorry for treating you the way that I have.'

A natural joy surged through her body and she leaped into his arms. Even if the anesthetic had worn off, he would have endured any ache for her love and comfort. Her love was stronger than any medicine a doctor would prescribe.

CHAPTER TWENTY-NINE

AFTER THE CAR wreck, he felt like a different man. Months ago, John took the ability to move without pain and aches for granted. Now, he prayed for his bones and joints to heal. When he walked, his limbs felt as though they really didn't belong to him. Each step was a negotiation. Yet, his life was in more order than it had been for the last decade.

Rachel assisted John in his rehabilitation. She reacted to his pain with as much thought and consideration as if she bore the discomforts herself. The journey truly humbled him.

When the doorbell rang, it surprised Rachel to find Bill with another older gentleman accompanying him.

"Good morning, darling," Bill said with a broad smirk. "Where is that son of mine?"

"In his study, making deals of course," she responded with a smile to match his. "Come on in."

"You didn't tell me John had become so progressive." Monty, the older gentleman, whispered to Bill as they walked through the house.

"What do you mean?" Bill said as his eyes narrowed towards Monty.

"Well, I didn't know he had married a black woman," Monty said in nearly a whisper.

"Hahaha married a black woman?" Bill repeated. "That's no wife. That's the nanny."

"Oh, well...the way she answered the door... she just seems so comfortable...and my kids had nanny's growing up, but they were never that attractive," Monty tried to ration.

"Stop being ridiculous," Bill declared in a hushed tone.

As they approached the study, John motioned for his father and Monty to enter as he wrapped a phone call.

"Hi dad," he replied with a grin which took Bill aback. The last time he remembered his son being thrilled to see him was many moons ago after one winning one of his Friday night varsity football games. "I did not know you'd be stopping by and bringing Uncle Monty with you."

Even though Monty Beale was not a blood relative, he had been Bill's attorney since John was a kid, so he referred to him as an uncle. He had practiced law for forty years. After completing law school at the University of Georgia, a young Monty set up shop on Peachtree Street where his office expanded over the decades.

Judge Clark Turner, a local district judge, proved to be a good friend throughout his career. In the past years, the judge helped Monty get started by appointing him in civil and criminal cases. Monty's reputation grew quickly in the community, and he was soon an established credible lawyer.

"I wish I could stand up and greet y'all, but moving hasn't been the easiest thing lately," John apologized for his lack of southern manners.

"Oh, that's okay, son," Monty said. "I'm just glad to see you back to business."

"What's with all these red ribbons placed on random things throughout the house?" Bill interrupted.

"Well, there's nothing random about it, dad," John replied. Leaning back in his chair and looking in the direction of the open door he yelled, "Rachel, could you come here!"

"Coming!" She replied.

"Could you explain to my dad the significance of placing the red ribbons?"

"Sure!" She said in a pleasant tone as she leaned against John's desk. "With the holiday season in full effect, I thought it would be nice to remind this very privileged family of gratitude. It can be so easy to slip into the mind state of "gimmie gimmie gimmie" while not being thankful for what you already have. Plus, I believe a happy soul is content with a normal and humble way of life. So, I've gone through the house and placed red bows on things such as light switches and couches with a note that says, 'Gifts God gives us are easy to overlook, so I've put a bow on them. He is so good to this family. Don't forget where these gifts come from.'"

"Isn't that so thoughtful and neat?" John said in awe.

"Yeah, real neat," Bill dryly responded.

"Well, John, I'm gonna go back to baking those sugar cookies for Sarah before it's time for me to go pick her up," Rachel said as she sensed Bill was not in the best moods.

"Okay, don't forget to put icing on mine," John playfully said.

"I won't," she said with a laugh as she walked down the hallway.

"So, she calls you John, huh?" Bill commented. "Kinda informal don't you think?"

"I'm not you, dad," John replied, still in good spirits. "So what brings you good men here?"

"Well," Monty answered as he took a seat. "I hate to be the bearer of bad news, even though I get paid very well to get people out of unpleasant situations, but the owner of the BMW has sued."

"Even though the car was abandoned?" John questioned.

"Property damage, son," Bill snapped. "How many times have I told you not to drink and drive? I can't believe you were that stupid!"

"Dad, I told you that I've turned over a new leaf. I'm done with drinking," John fired back.

"You? Quitting booze?" Bill comically said. "Ha! I'll believe that when I see it."

"Wow, thanks for the support, dad," John sarcastically said.

"Hey, c'mon gentleman," Monty spoke up. "What sense is there arguing over spilled milk? We can't do anything about the past, but fix it. Good thing it is only property damage which tends to be less costly because victims do not sustain any bodily injuries that need medical attention."

"Okay, well y'all didn't have to come over here to tell me that I will have to write a check," John said.

"Well, it's not that simple. Since you are the negligent party and you were driving under the influence, you can face jail time," Monty explained. "I've already filed an answer."

"Jail time?" John repeated.

"Yes! Jail time," Bill said, amused. "Do you think that you're above the law?"

"I never said that, dad," John firmly stated, annoyed by his father's tone. "I just never considered this whole ordeal could lead to incarceration."

"That's the problem," Bill shook his head. "You're letting that alcohol turn you plum stupid. You're going to rehab. I'm not going to let your bad press destroy my company."

"I told you, I'm clean, dad," John said, annoyed. "This whole house is dry. You can check if you want. Besides, I didn't ask for your help."

"You've been lying to me for years!" Bill shot back. "Now, all of a sudden you're supposed to be a new person. Ha! If it wasn't for my connections some judge would make an example out of you, boy."

"I'm gonna have to agree with your father," Monty intervened. "If this case gets in the wrong judge's hand, they would make an example out of you. In their eyes you're the poster child for what happens to spoiled brats when they grow up. Trust me, John. I can make this go away."

"This ain't up for debate," Bill harshly maintained. "Make it happen, Monty."

"Will do," Monty responded with a nod. "I'm playing golf with Judge Turner at noon, so we should get going. Nice seeing you, John."

"Yeah, same here," John replied, defeated. "I would see you fellas out, but of course, my condition won't allow that. Dad, please send mama my love."

"Alright, bye, son," Bill said before leaving.

After they were gone, John grabbed his cane and hobbled to the den where Rachel was.

"Geez, that seems like it was an intense meeting," she commented as he gently sat on the couch.

"You know, a fresh start is the weirdest thing," he said. "It's as if everything that happened to this point in time, was a prequel to what comes next. It feels as if that book closed, and a new one has opened. Yet, slowly but surely people, like my dad, won't allow me to start the new book. They keep bringing up the old story and all its chapters. All I want to do is right my past indiscretions and be a better man with each passing day. Sometimes I wonder if people will allow me to."

CHAPTER THIRTY

MAJORITY OF JOHN'S days were spent at home which gave him the much needed time to strengthen his relationship with Sarah. He did not understand how to improve his relationship with his daughter. Rachel minimized the shame he felt by suggesting he start by engaging in conversation. His reservations subsided when Sarah began confiding in him.

Every day after school they were eager to talk to each other. Amazed was an understatement when describing his reaction regarding her artistic capabilities. Guilt did not escape him and he often kicked himself for being a bad parent after each of their after school sessions. Each afternoon he proudly watched her draw and paint portraits.

On this day, a smile graced his face as he admired the facial features that she got from him and Anna.

"Daddy why are you smiling?" Sarah asked when she glanced back at him.

With a dip of his finger in the red paint, he playfully tapped her nose and tickled her. "Look at Rudolph getting into the Christmas spirit," he joked.

Rachel laughed as she watched them play and

felt blessed that God had given John a second chance to do right by his daughter. She thought they needed more time to be alone and bond, so she got up to leave. As she began to walk, a pillow flew across her face which was an invite in on the fun.

John and Sarah could not stop laughing as Rachel placed her hand on her hip with a smirk on her face. In retaliation, she grabbed a pillow and joined in the rumble.

Happiness overtook John, and he envisioned what life with Anna would have been.

After the excitement calmed, Sarah fell asleep while John and Rachel sat on the floor.

"I never knew you had such a good personality," John replied.

"Well, in your former life you did not seem like a joking man," Rachel said with a slight chuckle.

"Now that is a low blow, but I deserve it. Let's start off fresh and just tell me about yourself."

Rachel gazed at John intently to read him and see if he was sincere.

"What? Did I say something wrong? John asked.

"No, you didn't. I just had to examine your eyes because they never lie," she replied.

"That's amazing," John said, intrigued.

"I'm an amazing woman," she coyly responded with a smile. "But, why do you think I'm an amazing woman?"

"Well, my wife once told me the same thing about eyes," he answered perplexedly.

"I'm quite sure she was amazing," Rachel stated.

"Yes, she was, but what about you?" I sincerely want to know more about the woman who played a part in saving my life."

"I'm only doing what any person would do," she humbly replied. "And if you must know, I'm from a wealthy family. Similar to your dad, my father is a very busy and powerful man. I guess that's why I took such an instant liking to Sarah because in a way I could relate." With a wink and a nudge, she added, "Yet, growing up my daddy still found time for his baby girl."

"So you come from money?" He replied, shocked and confused. "Then why are you working as a nanny?"

"Well, if you must know," she answered with a sly grin. "My father owns the nanny agency that I work for. He wanted me to take an executive position, but my love for children won't allow that. I'd much rather be hands on. How else do you think I could afford to work a month free?"

"Yeah, I wondered about that," He chuckled.

"Also, I see this as a way for me to learn the business better with on-the-job training," she added.

"Yeah, I get that," he nodded. "When I first went to work for my dad, I insisted that I start at an entry-level position. I want to know the company from inside and out. Do you have any siblings?"

"More than I can count," she said with a grin. "As a matter of fact, one of my brothers will be in town during the holidays to meet with some of his associates."

"Feel free to invite him to the Christmas banquet I will host here at the mansion," John insisted.

"And just who will cater this Christmas banquet?" Rachel skeptically asked.

"'I was hoping you," he eased in jokingly.

"Oh, really?" She said as she placed her hands on her hips with an attitude.

"Okay, okay, I will take care of it," he smiled. "But I want to meet your brother and your father one day."

"You will, John," she spoke as she stood to walk out the room.

"Rachel," he called out.

"Yes," she answered as she turned around. "Thank you."

"For what?"

"For being you."

CHAPTER THIRTY-ONE

JOHN KISSED SARAH on the forehead before he walked out of the room to follow Rachel in the kitchen. Something fluttered in his stomach. It felt as though his heart danced around in his chest. He felt so light, like he was on top of the world. It was so strange. Strange to the point of frightening. Something was drawing him to Rachel other than her beauty.

It was a sense of completeness and peace. It was as if her aura was a mirror to Anna's because their beautiful souls were similar.

He reflected on the conversation he had with Anna and the phrase 'to love again' echoed repeatedly through his mind. Had she been referring to Rachel when she gave him the OK to love again?

When he entered the kitchen, he found Rachel washing plates. He could not help thinking of all the wonderful qualities she had. From the motherly instinct that Sarah needed, to the attention and affection she gave him even when he did not deserve it. Her beauty lit up the room and sparked the same feeling he had when he laid eyes on his late wife.

He picked up a towel and washed the last dish. "You know that I have a dishwasher, right?" He joked.

"So, I see that you are still in bright spirits," Rachel replied, surprised John was assisting her cleaning up because he had never done it before. "Dishwashers leave spots. My father always says if you're gonna do something, do it right."

"I can only hope that Sarah will talk about me the same way that you talk about your father when she becomes an adult," John warmly said.

"Well, he's an exceptional man," she replied with a smile.

"I can believe I've been a fool to miss out on Sarah's life," he stated as he handed Rachel the plate to put in the cabinet. "She is such a talented kid."

"You're making up for it now and that's what matters," Rachel responded. "Life is all about, loving your family, and enjoying their presence."

After a brief silence, he called out her name.

"Yes," she answered as she wiped off the countertop.

"When I tell you what I'm about to say, please don't think that I am crazy," John nervously explained.

The statement was enough to make Rachel stop cleaning and listen. "I don't believe in crazy, but go ahead, try me," she said.

"When I got into that accident," John slowly revealed. "I saw Anna."

He paused with the expectation to see a judgemental reaction. Satisfied that she did not judge him, he continued to detail his experience.

"John, all I can say is everything happens for a reason, and sometimes people cannot explain or fathom God's intent, but we must trust Him because it's for our good. Look at your experience as your greatest paradox, John."

"What do you mean?"

"Think about Anna's death. It nearly destroyed you, but you overcame it. Now you've got a second chance to not only make everything right between you and Sarah, but to possibly find love again."

In an instant, he sauntered up to Rachel and pulled her closer to him. He felt more alive than he had been in so very long. Before she knew it, he wrapped his arms around her. His embrace was warm and strong.

"I can't," she declared as she broke away.

"I don't know what got into me," he apologized, ashamed of the rejection. "It's too soon, right?"

"No, no. It's not that," Rachel responded.

"Then what is it?" John asked, confused.

"This is unprofessional," Rachel said before storming out of the kitchen.

CHAPTER THIRTY-TWO

JOHN PLACED HIS hand on his forehead as he sat at the table and realized that he had made a mistake. Meanwhile, Rachel laid on her bed and reflected on the kiss that was not supposed to happen even though she liked it very much. The only thing that could take her mind off the conflicting thoughts was a phone call to her cell-phone.

"Come outside."

"What?"

"You heard me, girl. Let me through this gate and get your butt down here."

Michael, her brother, drove a UPS truck up the driveway as she buzzed him in. He was cautious not to park in front of the house as he did not want to bring unwanted attention to them.

"Wow, you weren't kidding when you said this guy was loaded," he stated as he jumped out the truck.

"Michael, how long have you been here?" She spoke surprised.

"Nothing never surprises you, Rachel. What are you doing here?" He suspiciously asked.

"Uh, I hate when you redirect my questions

with one of your own," she responded annoyed. "And I don't like what your tone is implying. Anyway, what are you doing here?"

"It's the holidays," he flashed a megawatt smile. "Certainly, you had to know that I would be in town for the festivities" he answered. "Pops, phoned, and he said he wants you back home."

"I'm so tired of you bossing me around!" She declared loudly.

"Lower your voice," he said with a straight face. "That's daddy's directive which I support 100%."

"Well, I can't leave just yet," she responded.

"I think it's fair to say you're overstaying your welcome."

"Michael, I didn't plan to stay. I came here to do the work that needs to be done."

"I'd say the job is completed. In fact, it's been done for quite some time now. We got everything we needed. There's no reason for you to still be here."

"I just can't leave John –"

"Ah, like I already knew!" Michael said in outrage as a fire lit in his eyes. "He is your motive. It's probably foolish to ask if he knows who you are."

"He doesn't," she defensively shot back.

"Rachel, what are you doing?" He asked through clenched teeth as he took a step forward. "Are you waiting for him to find out? Or better yet, are you dumb enough to reveal your true identity?"

"I said I'd leave soon," Rachel replied with an attitude.

"What's holding you?"

"Well, I...I have something to finish."

"Man, you're really trying to blow our cover. This has never happened. Never! I should take you home tonight. I'm not so sure I can trust you."

"Michael, I told you, I can't leave yet," she pleaded as fear arose in her spirit. "The job isn't complete."

The sound of a dispatcher's voice through the truck's speaker paused their argument as Michael responded to the supervisor, who wondered where he was with the truck.

"Listen, I've gotta go," he informed Rachel. "Things are getting too risky for the both of us. For these next few days, don't let these so-called emotions that you think you're feeling, cloud your judgement. No matter how you feel, in the end we still have to split."

She rolled her eyes as her brother climbed into the UPS truck.

"Here," he added while handing her a package.

"What's this?"

"It's for the kid," he said with a grin. "And it's the perfect alibi just in case your boss is eavesdropping." With a stern look he added, "I'll see you in a few days."

CHAPTER THIRTY-THREE

"WAS THAT A delivery man out there?" John questioned when he met Rachel at the door.

She laughed inside because Michael's prediction had been right. John was snooping on their conversation from inside the house.

"Yeah, it's a package for our little angel, Sarah," she said with a faint smile as she put the present under the Christmas tree.

"That's odd," he said. "Didn't know they ran so late."

"Sarah's all tucked in the bed," she purposefully stated to divert John's current train of thought. "I think I'll hit the sheets as well."

She threw in an exaggerated yawn for extra effect as she walked up the stairs.

"Rachel, can we talk for a second?" John humbly asked as he limped behind her with his cane.

Without a word of acknowledgement, her walking tempo increased until she made it to her bedroom and slammed the door.

"C'mon, Rachel you just made a disabled guy chase after you," he said as he knocked on the door. "Please, have a heart."

After a moment of debating with herself about the most appropriate thing to do she let him in.

John entered the unlit room and turned on the lights. "Geez, when I had this house built I didn't realize that a grand staircase would one day leave me out of breath," he commented in an ill-fated attempt to break the ice.

She had might as well been a store mannequin as she lacked the high energy she typically displayed.

Sensing he had better get to the point before she kicked him out, John stated, "I think I owe you an apology, Rachel."

"And why is that?" She asked, frustrated.

"What I did was out of line and I shouldn't have crossed those boundaries," he sincerely expressed.

Unable to interpret her silence, he continued, "Um...I've never been very good at expressing my feelings. You know all about how Anna changed my life. I've never met a woman who shared her remarkable characteristics...until now. This past month you have shown me and my daughter a level of care and support that no one has shown me since my wife. You hold me accountable for my actions. You're easy to talk to. You always make me laugh; something I have not done in years."

John took a deep breath and smiled. "Ever since you've come into my life, joy has followed, which is why I know you are the one for me. Love radiates in your heart and spills out into the lives of all those around you. Not to mention you are drop dead gorgeous. That night of the accident when Anna came to me she told me that it's okay for me to love again."

Silence overtook the room as Rachel analyzed his eyes and studied every feature of his face.

"I don't know if you have a small feeling of the way I feel about you," John broke the silence as he grabbed her hand. "But, if you do… just know I care a great deal for you and I would be honored if you gave me the opportunity to be a part of your life."

"John! Stop," Rachel loudly pleaded.

"I'm sorry if I offended you Rachel, but I can't hide how I feel," he stated in a low tone that was a mixture of hope and frustration.

"But we can't feel this way toward each other," she reasoned.

"Is it because you work for me? If so, I technically fired you months ago," he said with a smile as he attempted to win her over.

"No, no. It isn't that," she answered with a pained expression on her face. "John, please drop this," she urged.

"Are you married or dating someone?"

"No."

"Well, is it because I'm white?"

"Your race has nothing to do with this," she frowned.

"Then what is it?"

"We just can't, okay," she said as she let go of his hand.

"At least give me a valid reason," John demanded.

"Well, Christmas is in two days and my father is expecting me to be home by New Year," she explained.

"Okay, so you're going home for the holidays to be with your family. What is the big deal?" His hands went up in exasperation.

"Look, there are some things that you just don't understand," she defensively said. "So, can you please leave?"

Rachel was overwhelmed and could not continue the conversation.

Unable to process what had transpired, John reluctantly granted her wishes and left the room.

CHAPTER THIRTY-FOUR

ONCE IN HIS bedroom, John laid down on his bed and pondered on the night's events as he stared at a picture of him and Anna on the night-stand. This was the first time he had expressed his feelings for another woman since her death and he could not believe she rejected him.

He wanted to gain closure about moving forward with his life. His tense nerves soon relaxed, his troubles, his pain melted away, and the surroundings disappeared, leaving him with thoughts of Anna and Rachel.

His head swam with half-formed regrets. It felt wrong that he cared for someone else, but he knew it wouldn't be long before those feelings turned into something greater. Rachel's lips were so gentle, so warm as their kiss grew heavier. His hands had slid off her face and tightened around her waist. There was no apprehension in his mind that he would have hungrily continued kissing her had she not pulled away.

Even though she did not admit to her feelings for him, there was no way she could deny it. He saw the way she bashfully looked at him at times. Sometimes the gazes were long, which revealed a lot. Sometimes they were quick glances that she did not think he caught. All of which made him even more unsure of how to win Rachel's heart.

"God," he said. "I know You sent Rachel in my life for a reason. You've got my attention, Father. What have I done to deserve all this turmoil and hurt I've gone through??? I do not want to sound ungrateful. You have given me a second chance to be a good father to Sarah. All I'm asking for is answers."

With a deep sigh, he got out of bed and tottered to the window. He gazed up at the sky as though answers were supposed to come down from the heavens.

Disappointed, he closed the curtains of the window. "I guess you saved my life only so I could raise my child alone."

John walked to the bed and laid down again. He looked at the portrait of him and Anna one more time, but this time the Bible that she used to read daily also garnered his attention.

He wondered how it had gotten on the nightstand because he had kept it in a bookcase that was solely for her books. "Rachel must have pulled it out," he guessed.

Nonetheless, he picked up the Bible and wiped the dust away with his hand as he opened it. The pages landed on the Book of James Chapter 1 and his eyes settled directly on Verse Two.

'Consider it pure joy, my brothers, whenever you face trials of many kinds, because you know that the testing of your faith develops perseverance. Perseverance must finish its work so that you may be mature and complete without lacking anything.'

He flipped the pages backwards as he became incensed at the fact of how God could want a person to endure hardship for the sake of maturing in their faith.

Eventually, he landed on Ephesians Chapter Two and saw that Verse Ten was highlighted, so he read it.

'For we are God's workmanship, created in Christ Jesus to do good works, which God prepared in advance for us to do.'

Slowly, the anger that he felt morphed into sorrow as he reread the scripture. He thought of the wealth he had amassed throughout the years as he read the passage with conviction. For so long he had held so much resentment towards God that it clouded his system of belief.

Immediately he cried out. "God I'm so sorry for ever questioning you. Thank you for your many blessings that I didn't deserve. Even through my success I still blamed you, but your grace and mercy intervened. I humbly come to you and ask for guidance."

John asked Jesus into his life and stayed up all night reading, studying, and gaining understanding of God's word.

CHAPTER THIRTY-FIVE

NATURE WAS ALWAYS a welcoming spirit to Rachel. The air was still. Stillness was what she needed to think about her next steps in life. She needed to feel connected to the Earth and get a grasp on her reality.

The woodland's floor was a million hues of brown, more than Rachel's eyes could detect. Mingled in were some stones, adding their grays to the mosaic beneath her feet. Some of the trees were khaki over the bark, kissed with moss. Forest animals seeking insects scarred other trees. Their injuries were mahogany and deep even where the sunlight reached them. The trees could feel something in her. Maybe it was her intuition.

The woodland flowed without the clocks of man. If it had not been for the faint sound of car horns honking on the streets nearby she would have forgotten she was in the city. She could not believe that John did not take advantage of his wonderful backyard more often.

"Rachel, is that you?" A voice called out.

It was the man she wanted to both see and avoid. He was the prime reason she took a stroll in the early morning. It was John.

"Good morning," she turned around and said with a smile she could not help hiding. "I didn't think I'd see you out here."

"Same here," he replied, hoping he did not sound giddy to see her.

"I have to tell you that your backyard is truly a gem," She gushed as they walked together.

"Really?" He commented, stunned by her amazement as he took his CD player earphones off.

"Nature is beautiful everywhere and we only have to open our eyes to that truth," Rachel replied.

"Just nothing but some dirt and grass that's good for a walking trail every now and then," he responded.

"Aw, John," she said, displeased. "You don't know what you have here."

"Well… I know I have you," he stated, hoping she would not run away. "I'm probably gonna sound like a broken record, but I'm sorry if I made you uncomfortable last night or even right now."

"It's okay, John," she calmly said. "Maybe it's time for me to resign. Move on to a new family. Maybe that will solve all our problems."

"I wouldn't call falling in love with each other a problem," he responded, annoyed.

"You can't deny that it's making things complicated between us," she pointed out.

"So, you do feel the same way I do," he said, overjoyed.

"John, let's not go there," she warned as she

turned to walk off.

"You can't keep running away from the way you feel about me," he said as he swiftly grabbed her arm. "Besides Anna, I've never met any woman like you before. You've given me hope and the inspiration to start living again. Before you came into my life, I was a walking zombie out to self-destruct."

"Believe me John there are plenty of good women out there," she discouragingly said. "You're just lonely and I'm here."

"Now, I'm offended," John scoffed. "You think my feelings for you are a joke. You're one of a kind. If there were plenty of good women out there, I would have bumped into her by now. You've allowed me to open myself up to you and now you want to shut me out?"

Tears built in Rachel's eyes as the chilly air reminded them both that it was winter.

"You know what? Just forget I ever was this honest with you," John responded out of frustration. "I'm done trying."

"No!" Rachel yelled.

"I've spilled my heart out to you already with less than the desired outcome I wanted. I'm done," John declared before limping off.

"John! John!" Rachel shouted as she caught up with him.

"There's nothing more to say, Rachel," he said while struggling to walk with his cane.

"I love you," she blurted.

"What did you say?" He asked in disbelief.

"I love you," she repeated in a small voice.

"I love you, too," he said as he used his free arm to embrace her.

CHAPTER THIRTY-SIX

JOHN AND RACHEL spent the next hour walking through the woodland with their arms intertwined. Even though his injured leg slowed them down, neither of them seemed to mind.

Rachel woke the pure side of John, his best side, all the facets of himself that only required love to be healthy and whole. If he had an eternity to be with her, he would sink into serenity, content in their closeness.

The further they delved into the conversation, the more their energy vibrated in such a unique way. Each the perfect complement of the other. They were truly smitten and falling more in love with one another by the minute.

"Look," she sadly said.

"The bird?" He whimsically questioned.

"Yes, the bird," she responded slightly peeved. "It's helpless and injured. We have to help it."

With her gloved hands, Rachel picked up the bird. "It can't fly. We have to take it to the animal rescue center."

He smiled because her unfailing kindness had won him over again.

"You're really quite wonderful, you know

that?"

"I'm doing nothing special, John," she replied as they walked to the house. "It's just human nature."

"It's never been in my character to be so concerned about another being, let alone an animal," he said as he tried his best to keep up.

"Giving is something we all grow into," she remarked. "Growing up, my father instilled in me that it is more blessed to give than to receive. So, it's not that you don't have it in you. It's just that you have not tapped into that side of yourself."

"I'll tell you one thing. If you didn't take such excellent care of Sarah, I'd say that you're in the wrong industry," he humorously said. "You're so motivational, you should be a speaker. It's very lucrative."

"Thanks," she said, flattered. "But, I could never leave the family business."

"And why is that?"

"Same reason you won't give up yours," she explained.

"Ouch!" He answered with a laugh. "Prior to meeting you, I would have never guessed that childcare could be such a profitable business. Are you guys just domestic?"

"No, my daddy was already international before I was even born," she acknowledged.

"Remarkable," John said as his eyes grew narrow. "What did you say his name was?"

"Has anyone ever told you that you're a handsome, yet inquisitive man?" She said with a smile.

"Haha, attractive I've heard a few times,

but nosy never," he laughed. "I can take a hint, though. I'll wake up, Sarah. She's never been to an animal rescue center before."

"Good idea," Rachel cheerfully answered, relieved the subject had changed. "I'll get a box to place the bird in and wait for you both.

CHAPTER THIRTY-SEVEN

CHRISTMAS EVE HAD finally arrived. Immersed in the holiday spirit for the first time in over a decade, John cooked breakfast.

"So, we have pancakes, sausages, and scrambled eggs," John said as he carried a pan around the kitchen table as he fixed each of them on a plate.

"Looks good, daddy," Sarah stated ready to devour the meal.

"Thanks, princess," he proudly beamed.

"I've never ever seen you cook before," she added in wonderment.

"Tis the season to be jolly," he sang, which caused Sarah to laugh.

"You're jolly because of Rachel, too," she teased.

"Haha, yes, and Rachel too," he laughed. "Are you okay with that?"

"Yes," she energetically answered. "I love Rachel. She's sooo nice, and fun, and oh yeah pretty too."

"I love her for those reasons, too" he smiled, glad his daughter approved of the relationship. "Go get her before breakfast gets cold."

As she bolted off, John asked what she wanted to drink.

"Apple juice!!!" She cheered.

John shook his head in delight as he thought about how he still loved apple juice over orange juice. He was amused that through genetics he handed down the love of the beverage to his daughter.

"Mmmm...smells good!" Rachel said as Sarah playfully pulled her into the kitchen.

"Good morning, beautiful," John responded as he pulled her chair out for her to sit."

"John!' She blushed and lifted her eyebrows in Sarah's direction.

"It's okay, I already know," Sarah said before sipping more apple juice.

"John, you told –" His head nod cut her off.

"I love you Rachel and I'm so glad that my daddy does too," Sarah smiled.

"I love you, too," Rachel walked over to Sarah's seat. "In fact, I fell in love with you first."

Sarah smiled. She had never known motherly love and now since she had it, she never wanted to lose it.

John placed Sarah's plate on the table and pulled out her chair and repeated the same act with Rachel.

"Thank you!" Rachel cheerfully said.

"You're welcome," he replied as he turned to Sarah. "Always remember if a man doesn't seat you Princess, he isn't a gentleman, and he doesn't deserve you."

"Daddy," Sarah replied, slightly embarrassed.

"But, you have a long time to worry about that. Don't you?" He joked and gave her a kiss on the forehead.

"Eat up, baby," John said as he took a seat.

"Hold up," Rachel urged. "Now, yall know we need to say grace."

Sarah begged to bless the food, which John and Rachel agreed. They joined hands and ended her sweet prayer with an amen. A permanent smile stayed plastered on her face as she ate.

Throughout the meal, Rachel glanced at John and Sarah. They were finally happy, but she was so torn. Certain things needed to happen, and her loving them both was not part of the plan.

"How will I ever make this work?" She wondered.

"Do you like it?" John asked as he noticed she looked absent-minded.

"Oh yes, where are my manners? It's delicious," Rachel replied as she was knocked out of her thoughts.

"I know I may have lost my way around the kitchen, but some things I just can't forget," he responded.

"What else do you know how to cook?" She asked.

"I'm afraid my cooking skills are limited to this one dish," he replied with a loud chuckle.

She couldn't hold back her laughter and neither could Sarah. "Looks like I'll still be doing most of the cooking," Rachel added.

John could watch her smile all day, and he was intent on winning her heart forever.

"Tonight we are having a Christmas Eve dinner and since you mentioned that your brother was in town, I was hoping you could invite him."

"I'll see if he is available," Rachel replied.

"Great, I can't wait to meet him," John responded as he got up from the table. "Oh yeah, before I forget, I bought you a dress that I would love for you to wear to the party. That's if you like it."

"As long as it isn't too revealing," Rachel responded with a slight attitude.

"Ha! That's one reason I love you. You are a woman with class," John responded as he got up to put the dishes away.

"'Rachel, I hope I wasn't out of line for buying you the dress," John apologized. "I just thought about how that must have came across."

"No, John, it's fine," she answered. "But, I have something to talk to you about."

"Woah, this sounds serious," he said.

Hesitant to answer, she just smiled. He attempted to pry information from her, but failed and gave up.

"I have some late gifts to get, so I'm about to do some last minute shopping. Do you need anything while I'm out?

"No, I'll be fine."

Chapter Thirty-Eight

RACHEL AND SARAH spent most of the afternoon goofing off and playing around on the piano. Sarah had fooled her piano instructor into believing that she was disinterested in the lessons, but she loved playing the instrument and relished in showing off to Rachel.

She had inherited a competitive streak from her grandfather and egged on Rachel to compare who could play the piano the best.

"I bet you the last fudge brownie that you can't play better than me," she teased.

Similar to her, Rachel had spent many years of her childhood mastering the basics of the piano.

"I may be rusty, but I do love delicious fudge brownies," Rachel joked as she playfully scooted Sarah off the bench and began to slowly play Gershwin's "Rhapsody in Blue".

She was surprised that she remembered every note because she had not played much since she was little. As her confidence grew, she played several different scales by heart one after the other. Years of practicing had imprinted the notes and techniques so deeply in her fingers' memory that they instantly knew what to do.

"Wow, how did you remember if you haven't played in so long?" Sarah asked.

"Well, sweetie, there are some things that you never forget," Rachel answered.

"When I grow up, I wanna be just like you," Sarah said in adulation.

"No, you don't. You wanna be your own person," Rachel explained. "There's nothing that I can do, that you can't do."

"Sounds like something my Nana would say," Sarah giggled. "Can we do something helpful today?"

""What do you mean?" Rachel asked.

"Like give away some money or clothes," she answered. "I'm trying to make sure God sees me, so He can bless me. I don't want any bad stuff happening to me. My Nana says if I don't do a lot of good things, God won't see me and I will get lost in the shuffle."

"Hahaha sure. But, I want you to know that God always sees you, sweetie," Rachel explained. "You don't have to do things to get His attention. You already have it. He's just waiting on you to get to know him."

"Really?" Sarah wondered. "With all the people in the world I don't see how that is possible?"

"Well, He made all of us and His son Jesus took care of that 'big shuffle' your grandma told you about when he died for all of us."

"How?"

"Well, his death offered us freedom from judgment forever," she informed her. "So, you see, you can't buy or bribe your way to heaven by doing good things. You have to believe in God and accept his son Jesus Christ."

"Isn't that why people get baptized?"

"Yep."

"Well, can we do that today?" She asked, wide-eyed.

"Haha, you'll have to ask your father, girl," Rachel laughed.

CHAPTER THIRTY-NINE

JOHN WAS ONE of many who walked through the crowd with a mission of getting last-minute presents. Even though he had gotten plenty of gifts for the special women in his life, he wanted to make sure he had overlooked nothing. Usually, he spent the holiday in his office. But this year he preferred to be a part of the festive elation.

He could hear bells at the corner of the clothing store he planned on entering.

"Happy holidays! Happy holidays!" A homeless man excitedly repeated as everyone walked by him like he didn't exist. He had a pan sitting in front of him with a few dollars in the middle.

The closer John came to the store, the bell became more familiar. The sound triggered his memory and traveled back in time to a moment with Anna.

"John, we can't let her sleep in the cold, it's 15 degrees outside," Anna said as they sat at a red light.

A homeless woman stood at the street corner

and screamed, "Happy Holidays!" At the top of her lungs as she rang a bell.

"She isn't our problem, babe," he responded, annoyed by Anna's good-nature. "Whatever bad choice she has made in her life is the reason she is in her current situation."

The moment that statement left his mouth, Anna grew angry and reached for her coat that laid on the back seat.

"What do you think you are doing?" John said, bewildered that he was actually arguing with his wife about a homeless woman.

"I can't believe you would actually be that inconsiderate and not have any compassion for her!" Anna's temper flared. "She is still a human being and if you feel that way then I'll be outside with her!"

John could not believe his eyes when she got out of the car to stand with a homeless stranger in the freezing weather.

"You can't be serious?!" John yelled out of the car window. "The light just turned green for Pete's Sake."

The car behind them honked their horn. John looked out of the rearview mirror and saw a lengthy line of cars. In a split second, he decided to turn and pullover at the curve where the homeless woman and now his wife stood. Never once did she worry about John leaving her. After all, she was six months pregnant with his child.

Anna introduced herself to the woman, and started up a friendly conversation.

"Okay, okay. You've got my attention," He

frustratingly admitted. "Now, can you please get in the car?"

Anna did not budge as she stubbornly stood her ground.

"Both of you!" He yelled out the window.

Anna had gotten her way and smiled. She turned to whisper something to the woman, and they packed her things. Reluctantly, John got out of the car and helped them load the trunk. To appease his wife, he paid for a one week hotel room for the woman.

When they drove off Anna looked at John from the passenger seat. "John," she softly said his name.

"Yes, dear," he answered with a deep sigh.

"I want you to always remember, love bridges the gap amongst people."

"Why are you telling me this, Anna?"

"Because people make bad choices in life and we shouldn't hold that against them," she defensively answered.

John turned into a Kroger shopping center and parked the car. He stared blankly at Anna because he did not understand what he deemed as her being dramatic.

"If God can forgive us and show compassion, then why can't you?" She questioned.

"I'm not God, babe," he painstakingly answered. "Forgive me for being concerned about the well being of my family."

John opened his car door to go into the store. "Love your neighbor as yourself. Love does no harm to its neighbor," she stated.

She grabbed his arm and reached across him to close the door.

"Look, Anna, I can love the next person, neighbor, or whatever you want to call them all I want, but it still won't change a thing because still to this day, I never received your Father's blessing," John jeeringly said.

"Love is patient. Love is kind," she said, quoting another scripture out of the bible.

"I don't know if it's the pregnancy hormones or the fact that it is Christmas, but you're really becoming insufferable, Anna. For the sake of a peaceful night, can we please just drop this?"

"Sure, John," Anna neutrally replied. "One day, you will see what the power of love can do."

John recalled his late wife's words and smiled. "Sir, could I possibly bless you this Christmas?" He asked the man who rang the bell.

The man looked around to be certain John was speaking to him. "Well as you can see blessings don't come often to me," he said. "So I appreciate anything."

"It's too cold to be out here and the temperature is dropping, allow me to get you a room in a hotel," John replied as he rubbed his leather gloved hands together.

"Stop joking, man. Enjoy your holiday," the man laughed at him.

"I'm not joking, sir, and if you would allow me, I would like to buy you some clothes and shoes. All you have to do is step inside the store with me," John explained as he saw the man wasn't convinced.

As the man walked towards the store entrance, he asked why John was being so nice to him. "My wife taught me a long time ago to have compassion just the way God has for us," John explained.

"Then your wife is an angel," the man smiled. "God bless you both and thank you."

As John opened the door for the man, he grinned and replied, "I guess you are right. She was my angel."

CHAPTER FORTY

THE SPIRIT OF celebration filled the mansion. The house had not thrived with vibrancy since Anna's passing. Guests composed of associates, employees, and clientele who were all invited by John. Family and friends were sent an invitation, but they all declined because they felt that he was still a pain of a man.

All those in the present company had only attended the dinner party because of John's business acumen, but mostly for the Christmas gifts. Despite his often rude disposition, last year he bought all the employees apple watches. This year they waited patiently to see what he would give them.

His gracious transformation shocked everybody. They were used to a man who tried his best to avoid them daily. Now, he walked around, shook their hands, and thanked everyone for their attendance.

To his surprise, his father was in the crowd. John made his way toward Bill. The usual handshake he expected from his son was replaced by a full on bear hug, which caught him off guard.

"What's all this for?" Bill asked.

"Thank you for being you," John said with a wide grin.

"You're w-w-welcome," Bill stuttered, unsure of how to respond. "Something is different about you, son?"

"I know. God has shown me new light, dad. I have so much to live for."

As he spoke, the diamond earrings and bracelet he gifted Rachel illuminated as she walked down the stairs in the long white silk Dior dress he had picked. Her glow was indescribable.

"I'm just missing one thing," John slowly said as Rachel's beauty caused him to stumble.

"Don't tell me - " Bill muttered as he shook his head.

"You better believe it," John smiled as he met her at the bottom of the staircase.

Bill stood in disbelief as the guest watched in awe.

"No wonder he's been in a better mood lately," one of the male employees joked.

"I would have never guessed John was down with the swirl, but since he is I will put in my bid if things don't work out between them," one of the female employees laughed.

"You are truly an angel," John commented as he reached for Rachel's hand to help her down the last step.

"Well, thank you," she responded with a forced smile. "You are quite a charmer."

"Come say hi to my dad," John merrily said as he led the way.

After the re-introduction, they both noticed a

look of disapproval on Bill's face.

"I think I see my brother, Michael," she suggested, happy to escape the awkwardness that Bill had created.

"What is your problem, dad?" John demanded.

"I've already met and talked to Rachel," he snapped. "Nothing to see here."

"What do you mean there's nothing to see here?" John questioned.

"She's the help!" He grumbled. "I thought I taught you better than that, son. To make matters worse, she is black and people like her are only after your money, John!"

At that moment, Rachel and Michael overheard Bill's remark and were disgusted. Michael wanted to punch Bill out, but Rachel held him back.

"I detest you for spewing such hate, dad. Rachel is a beautiful woman. If you would get to know her, then you would know that she has her own money. Now excuse me, I have a party to host."

John turned around to see Rachel's eyes filled with tears. The hurt she felt from Bill's words was written all over her face. "C'mon, Michael, there's no reason for us to stay here," Rachel stated as she grabbed her brother's hand and maneuvered through the crowd.

As soon as John ran behind them, the co-host of the party asked John to join in on addressing the guest. Always understanding of his duty as a host, he stopped and joined in on the festivities. His interest in the celebration had deflated, and he was ready to send everyone home. Refraining from anger as best he could, he slowly grabbed the mic as people quieted down.

"Thank you, everybody, for coming out tonight to celebrate the holidays. I had a speech prepared, but I don't think I'll be using it tonight. I want to be honest and share something with you guys. Ten minutes ago, if someone would've asked me who I respected most, I would've said, my father. Now, I can't say that and it saddens me."

John's eyes searched the crowd until he found his father. He wanted to see his father's blood boil regarding the statement.

"Don't worry, dad. I won't tell these lovely people what you said. I just want you all to know that I can no longer work for a man with bigoted values."

A big gasp could be heard from the crowd. Guests were shocked and could not suppress their whispers and mumblings. Everyone attempted to gain clarity about his statement.

"What I am saying is I will be resigning as Vice President of Better Life Insurance company."

"This is absurd!" Bill screamed from the crowd before he turned to leave.

"Oh yeah, one more thing, there is an envelope for every employee with a $2,000 check. Enjoy the rest of the party. Merry Christmas, folks!"

CHAPTER FORTY-ONE

"SEE, I WARNED you this guy was no good," Michael stated in a know-it-all tone.

"Ssssh," she said as she listened to John wrap up his speech from her room. "If you would listen, then you would hear that he just quit his job for me. He loves me."

At first, she planned on leaving, but John stirred her spirit after he stood up to his father in front of all the guests.

"I don't understand you, girl, you're risking everything we have to be a part of a family where you won't have full acceptance!" Michael shouted. "If I can't talk any sense into you, daddy can. Let's go!"

"Leave me alone!" She screamed.

A tug-of-war battle ensued between Rachel and Michael over one of her suitcases.

"Hey! Let it go!" John charged as he ran into the room, which caused Michael to lose his grip on the suitcase.

"I'm talking to my sister," Michael sternly replied.

"Michael, please," Rachel pleaded.

"I can't believe this," Michael retorted. "I'm

done. Do what you wanna do."

As he walked out of the room, John consoled an emotional Rachel.

"I love you, John," she cried.

"I love you," he replied while wiping her tears.

He saw that the open suitcase was filled with clothes which made him light heartedly ask if she was really trying to leave him. After she didn't answer him, he explained, "My father's ignorance shocked me too. I know my dad is from the old school, but somehow I thought that he would not be closed towards our relationship. He has issues within himself that he has to deal with. I realize nobody is perfect, but I do not condone hatred of any kind."

"You're right, it takes growth," she answered while still in his arms. "When I first met you, I would have never imagined that we would have the relationship that we do now. Nevertheless, I must leave."

Rachel broke out of their embrace and started packing her suitcase.

"I don't understand," John said, unable to hide his devastation. "What about us? What about Sarah? This will break her heart."

"'I know," she sobbed. "But, it has to be this way."

"Besides this minor hiccup with my father, everything is going good with us. I don't understand. How am I supposed to live without you?" He asked while he fought back tears.

"It's not my choice," she said as tears poured down her face.

"It is your choice! You have a choice! Is it your brother?! Is it your father!?" John said as his temper flared.

"Yes...and...no," Rachel indecisively answered.

"Well, which one is it?!" He demanded. "You just told me you love me. None of this makes sense. You are the woman whom I've been searching for."

"My father will disown me, John and I can't live with that!" She shouted.

"But, what about me disowning my father for you?" He snapped. "Is love not enough?"

Rachel looked at him blankly as she wiped her face.

"So, is this what you had to tell me the other day? Were you planning to leave all along? Were you just going to use your brother as the scapegoat the entire time?" He drilled.

"It's not like that, John," she cried. "You'll never understand."

"I'm asking you to explain!" He yelled. "Maybe my dad was right about you!"

Before Rachel knew what happened her hand had slapped John's face, which was now red.

"I guess your true colors are showing now," she remarked. "My brother came here to take me back home. I think that's the best thing to do right now."

"I can't believe this," John shook his head. He could not believe how he chose her over his father, but she couldn't do the same for him. "Well, if you want to leave you know where the door is."

She walked towards the door with her luggage and stopped. She turned to face him and stated, "Trust God. Don't lose your faith because this is only the beginning to what He has planned for you. Goodbye, John."

A look in her direction would bring out mixed emotions that John was not prepared to handle, so he thought it would be best to not make eye contact with her.

CHAPTER FORTY-TWO

OUT OF NOWHERE, it was as though Rachel had disappeared. Through the guest room window, John wanted to watch her leave even though it would hurt him. Usually, she parked out front, but he could not identify her car from the line of others.

After all the love they had professed and the plans they had made, he couldn't believe she left him so easily. He did not know whether to laugh or cry because for the first time in a decade he had fallen in love, been vulnerable and considered a second chance at life.

The smell of the soft fragrance she wore lingered in the air, which reminded him of the dreary times he went through mourning the death of Anna. Since he had grown stronger over the last few months, backpedaling to his old ways was not an option. People still celebrated downstairs, so he joined the party.

Music blasted from speakers as he walked into the den. Sarah sat all alone. Because of her height, her legs dangled while her face rested in the palm of her hands. The grown-ups bore her to death.

"Can I get this dance?" John asked with a

smile.

"Daddy, I don't know how to dance like old people," she replied.

"Old people?" He laughed. "Well, it's simple." He counted and snapped his fingers at the same time. "You go 1-2-3. 1-2-3." He took her by the hand and led by example, teaching her the steps.

"Daddy?"

"Yes, princess?"

"Why did Rachel leave with her suitcases? "

The question took John by surprise and he nearly paused him in motion. Her observation confirmed that Rachel had slipped by him, but he did not know how she did it so fast.

"Well, she had to go home, princess," he struggled to answer.

"Is she coming back?"

"I really hope so," he said in denial. "But I'm afraid she won't."

"She told me to tell you that God loves us so much and that He sent his angels to watch over us," Sarah mentioned,

John stopped dancing and looked at Sarah with a surprised expression.

"She told you that?" He asked.

"Yes, and she said to keep Him first in everything you do and you will prosper," she informed him.

"I'm gonna miss her so much, daddy," she sighed. "I can tell her my deepest darkest secrets and she always tells me good things, especially about God. We've gotta get her to come back, daddy."

"That has to be her choice," he remarked. After briefly contemplating Rachel's whereabouts in his mind, John realized that Sarah had begun to cry. He wiped under her eyes with his handkerchief and energetically said, "Come on, let's dance!"

John lifted Sarah off the floor and showered her with hugs and kisses before they started to dance as the live band performed. Photographers could not resist snapping shots of the candid moment to print in the Atlanta Journal Constitution.

CHAPTER FORTY-THREE

EVEN THOUGH RACHEL'S DEPARTURE LEFT JOHN heartbroken, his determination to make Christmas special for Sarah was undeterred. A pile of wrapped presents overflowed from under the immaculate decorated tree.

Before the fun began, John felt it was necessary to tell her why Christmas was a cause for celebration. "This is the day we celebrate the birth of Jesus. His parents were given gifts when he was born, so we carry on the tradition with our own children," John informed her. "So, when you open these gifts, know that Jesus loves you very much."

"Daddy, you sound like Rachel," she smiled.

He agreed that Rachel had rubbed off on him during her brief time with them. But she was the last thing he wanted to discuss. After he danced with Sarah, he realized that the bond fathers and daughters share are one of a kind. Now, he cherished their relationship and would let nothing come between them. Even though it pained him, he understood Rachel's motives for leaving.

"Princess, I'd like for you to open this first," John excitedly said.

Sarah's heart pounded with anticipation. "Okay, I wonder what it is!" She exclaimed, which caused her golden ringlets to bounce up and down.

In no time, she unwrapped the gift to discover a bundle of unlabeled VHS tapes. "Thanks, daddy, but we have TiVo now. I don't have to use video-tapes to record my favorite shows anymore."

John laughed and explained that the tapes were not blank and asked Sarah to push one in the VCR. Even though she rolled her eyes and wondered if her father had gone mad, she fol-lowed his instructions. It took a minute for the squiggly lines to go away once she pressed play.

"Geez, daddy how old is this tape?" She joked.

The picture cleared up and Sarah watched in amusement as a boyish man with a backward baseball cap danced.

"Daddy...is that you?!" She asked once the moving image spoke.

He raised his eyebrows and half-grinned, "Don't judge me."

"Wow, you were so young!" She noted.

As the home movie played, a youthful John kissed a woman who had her hair in a messy ponytail. Sarah looked back at her father and play-fully rolled her eyes. When the camera zoomed out, the pretty lady had on a crop top that left her bare tummy exposed.

"We will spoil this baby rotten, John," the woman smiled.

"Yep, and the baby will inherit your sweet tooth," he laughed as he placed his hand on the woman's belly. "What are you craving now?"

"Pepperoni and pineapple pizza," she giggled.

A beam of joy dashed inside of Sarah as tears filled her eyes. She realized the young woman on the screen was her mother. "We sound alike when we laugh," she proudly pointed out. "And we have the same dimple on the left side when we smile."

Tears rolled silently down John's face as the emotions of seeing his daughter and deceased wife reunite in spirit overtook him. On the screen, Anna's face was just as pretty as the first day he saw her. Now, Sarah's eyes twinkled with laughter and her teeth glistened when she smiled as she realized the similarities shared with her mother.

The camera zoomed in on Anna as she said, "To my unborn child, mommy loves you so much. I can't wait to hold you in my arms and kiss your tiny face."

Sarah hugged her father and thanked her for the gift she always wanted. "Finally, I have a piece of my...my…"

"It's okay to say it, princess," John rubbed his fingers through her hair.

After a deep sigh, Sarah confidently said, "Finally, I have a piece of my mom!"

"That's right! You no longer have to feel ashamed about your mama not being here with us," he stated. "I've been selfish all these years because I kept all those memories of your mother bottled up inside. I love her so much. But, now it's time to share those good times with you. I hope you treasure these tapes for the rest of your life."

"I will daddy! I will," she proclaimed as she gave him a kiss on the cheek.

After they finished watching the tape, John reminded Sarah she had other gifts to open before she began looking at another home movie. It was hard to lure her away, but she wanted to see what other surprises laid under the tree.

"Look, daddy, it's a gift for me from Rachel," Sarah excitedly announced as she held up the wrapped present.

John placed his cup of coffee on a coaster and made his way to Sarah. "Well...open it," he curiously responded.

"OK, OK, just chill, dad," she laughed while opening the attached card. "You are truly a blessing to your father and he loves you dearly, as I've told you before," she read aloud. "I promised to be your kitchen guide, but this will have to do for now. Just follow the directions and you will have the head chef position in your father's kitchen. Merry Christmas, my beloved. Love Rachel."

Sarah ripped the package open and discovered a cookbook. "Thank you!" She held the book tight to her chest and spun around.

Unable to stomach Rachel's generosity because he had not dealt with the recent heartache she had inflicted on him. John walked away.

"Aren't you going to open up your gift, Daddy," Sarah asked as she ran up to him with a card and package.

"It's from me and Rachel," she said with a

smile.

John took the gift and opened the card. Before he read, he tried to prepare himself the best he could. Unsure of the level of intimacy, elected to silently read the card.

My Dear John,

When you show a person a part of themselves they've been suppressing or denying, they either have an emotional breakthrough or submit to their primitive anger response. In your case, I saw emotional development. I pray by now you have grasped my motive for leaving. There was no way possible I could stay no matter what I attempted to do. I had no choice. My father wanted me home, and I had to go. Look at it like this. The love Sarah has for you is the same that I have for my father, but on a greater scale because our bond is far stronger. It took everything in me to walk away, but I know my father and he would've sent for me. But this isn't

forever because you will see me again, trust me. Set yourself free. You owe yourself that much.

Love again.
I love you, Rachel.

At the bottom of the card, she scrolled her signature and wrote, 'Hebrew 13:2' beneath it. He hurriedly walked to the study where he kept his bible and thumbed through the pages until he located the scripture.

"Do not forget to entertain strangers, for by so doing some people have entertained angels without knowing it."

His eyes scanned the page, and he read the passage again. His mind swarmed with thoughts. First, Anna had summoned him to love again during their heavenly exchange. He couldn't believe Rachel had said the exact thing. To add to these coincidences, she directed him to a bible verse. "It couldn't be," he mumbled under his breath.

"What's wrong?" Sarah asked.

"Nothing, princess," he answered, trying to maintain his composure. "Sometimes, God sends people in our lives for a season. We're closer and better people because of Rachel."

"We sure are, daddy!" She smiled. "Now, can you open my gift, daddy," she urged as she handed him a large folder.

He slowly undid the clasp and his eyes watered at the sight of a portrait of him and Rachel.

"I drew it, daddy! Do you like it?"

"I love it, princess. You captured the angel God sent us."